RECKLESS

Lori Bell

This book is a work of fiction. Names, characters, places and incidents are the product of the author's imagination or are used fictitiously. Any resemblance to actual events, locales, or persons, living or dead, is coincidental.

Copyright © 2016 by Lori Bell

All rights reserved. This book or any portion thereof may not be reproduced or used in any manner whatsoever without the express written permission of the publisher except for the use of brief quotations in a book review.

Cover photograph by Lori Bell
Photographed on the cover, Michael Bell

http://www.justanswer.com/medical/2cc7v-good-blow-head-forehead-right-eye-area.html
https://en.wikipedia.org/wiki/Opioid_overdose

Printed by CreateSpace

ISBN 978 1539806806

DEDICATION

A lifelong bond? Or a lesson learned.

Everyone we have ever met in our lives and held onto will exist as one of those.

Some relationships are not meant to be. Others are either effortless or ultimately strengthened from weathering storms.

This book is dedicated to those of you who know how to let go, and when to hold tighter.

Chapter 1

The tires on the full-size silver pickup truck crushed the rocks underneath them as Tate Ryman drove on the driveway that led up at least two-hundred yards to the detached double-car garage. He hit the brakes as he waited for one of the white carriage-style garage doors to lift. When he pulled his truck inside, he didn't bother to close the garage door again. He just stepped out into the cold outside air and inhaled a long, slow breath through his nostrils. It was freezing and the wind in his face was brutal. But not nearly as brutal as what he had just gone through.

Tate's tan work boots, laced up over his ankles, stepped on the rocks outside of the garage as he walked the path up to the house. That one-hundred-year-old, refurbished two-story house had snow white siding, cobalt blue window shutters, and four matching round pillars under the wraparound porch with a high roofed overhang. The brisk wind cut right through his faded denim. He could have used a coat layered overtop his navy blue and green flannel shirt, which was left untucked and flapping at the ends in the wind.

The entry door to the mudroom was unlocked and Tate stepped inside. He bent over to untie his boot laces, and then slipped out of them right there on the middle of the floor. He left the boots and moved up the two steps which led into the kitchen. His thick white socks on the cream tiled floor felt comfortable and warm. This was the first warmth his body had felt in hours. Tate knew he was chilled to the bone. Raw emotion, not just the weather, was to blame for that feeling.

The kitchen was dark as the overcast sky wasn't providing any direct sunlight in the window above the stainless steel sink. Tate instantly smelled the coffee aroma. He looked on the counter and noticed the full, fresh-brewed pot. "Edie?" he called out, but it wasn't his girlfriend of two years, who lived there with him, that came around the corner and stood in the kitchen doorway.

Physically, Edie Klein was every man's fantasy. Tall, shapely, blonde, and flawlessly beautiful. The first time Tate had laid eyes on her at a local bar in downtown Camden, Delaware, he looked twice and he stared long. And so did every other man in the room. Tate never thought a woman like her would give him a second glance, but she had.

"Syd? What are you doing here?" Tate watched her flip the light switch on the wall. A frosted glass fixture that hung under a ceiling fan above the round wooden kitchen table lit up the room. Sydney Klein stood a fair distance away, wearing an oversized pale pink hoodie, a pair of baggy stone-washed jeans, and white tennis shoes. Tate could not ever remember seeing her with anything else on her feet except for white tennis shoes, any time of year. She was about three inches shorter than her sister and her shoulder-length auburn hair was considerably plain in comparison to Edie's long blonde tresses. They were night and day –in appearance and personality– for sure.

"I thought you could use a friend," Syd answered, making brief eye contact with him before she made herself useful and walked over to the countertop to pour coffee into the empty glass mugs she already had sitting out.

"Did Edie call you?" he asked, assuming so. They were sisters, but really not at all close.

"She texted, and said you would be here–"

"Alone? Because she's tied up at work?" Tate wasn't surprised. But, he had reached out to his girlfriend, and a part of him did hope she would put him first this time. Just this once. After all, he did just lose the greatest man he ever knew.

"She'll be here," Sydney defended her sister.

"Right," he agreed, pulling out a chair from under the table when she placed both of the steaming coffees down. His on the far end of the table, and hers on the complete opposite. She never did sit close. She always kept just enough distance between herself and this man. And she had her reasons. "Thank you," he smiled at her, and Sydney glanced down at her black coffee before she looked at him again. His sandy-brown hair was growing out a little around his ears and over his eyebrows. His blue eyes looked sad. *Of course he was sad.*

They shared silence while they each took a few sips of their coffee. And then Tate started to open up to her. Sydney was too introverted to pry. But, she knew Tate would eventually talk to her. He always did. They were like two old friends with an easy connection. Tate was more likely to embrace that concept than Sydney. As strange as it seemed, each time she was with him, it felt as if she was starting all over to get up the nerve to talk to him. Really talk to him. But today, especially today, she was trying harder to feel at ease. He was hurting, and she felt pained just looking at him, watching him, listening to him speak.

"He went peacefully," Tate began. "It's just a damn shame that he had to suffer at all to begin with. I mean, Alzheimer's is just brutal. I think he did know we were there at the end. Mom believes that anyway, and Kathy." Tate's older sister, Kathy had been the only one to cry when her father left this world. Rex Ryman's wife just held his hand a little tighter, encouraging him every inch of the way to *just go.* And Tate only sat there, close by, feeling both pained and numb at the very same time, if that were possible. *His father was gone.*

Sydney was sympathetic. She slowly shook her head. "Is there anything I can do?" she asked, believing her sister was rotten to her core for not being there for this man. Edie should have been beside Tate at his dying father's bedside this morning. If she loved him, she would have.

"Keep the store afloat, as you always do," he genuinely smiled at her. "I'll be gone for a few days, at least until the funeral is over and I'm sure Ma will have a few things for me to help her with."

"You can count on me for that," Sydney said, knowing she was about to double her hours at Ry's Market downtown where she had been employed through high school and ever since she graduated eight years ago. She was *just a cashier*, as Edie enjoyed pointing out to her, but her knowledge of the store reached far beyond checking out shoppers at the register. The Rymans had been good to her. They hired her and she was in their lives long before Edie came on the scene and charmed her way into Tate's life. And into his bed. She had his heart, that was for certain, as Sydney or anyone else could plainly see. No matter how reckless Edie was with Tate's feelings, he looked past all of it. He would do absolutely anything for her.

Tate's livelihood had been construction. He was a man who needed to work with his hands, but he had spent the last year and a half managing the store for his ailing father. Rex and Mary Lou Ryman owned Ry's Market and whether he wanted to or not, Tate now managed it. His sister, ten years older, who had moved to Florida with her attorney husband and two babies more than a decade ago, wanted no part of it. Except for her share of the stock. Tate loathed being the store manager, but he had done it for his parents. Now that his father was gone, Tate had a decision to make. A decision that he knew would break his seventy-five-year-old mother's heart. Their store was a part of her and always would be. But, it wasn't a draw for Tate. He didn't feel a love for the family business pumping through his veins. For him, being in charge of a market –where scheduling, payroll, ordering groceries, catering, and meeting customer service needs were a part of his everyday routine- felt mundane. Tate preferred the challenge of constructing buildings from the ground up with his bare hands. And he refused to live his life, day in and day out, growing old inside of that market. Just like his father had.

"Syd, between us," Tate said, leaning forward, hovering over his coffee cup, with both of his masculine hands curled around it. Sydney stared at those hands. The hands of a hard-working man. The hands she, long before her big sister ever met that man, had wanted to hold and to feel. Sydney could still remember the first time she saw Tate Ryman. He would come into the market sometimes, and she floated on air each and every time. She was sixteen years old then. And now, at twenty-six, that feeling remained. Stronger than ever. It was like a staple in her heart. "I want you to take over. Be the store manager. For chrissakes, Syd, you know the place inside out. Better than me or anyone else now."

Sydney blushed. He was talking crazy. He was grieving for his father. There was no way Tate could have been serious. He could not have meant what he said. *I want you... to take over. Be the store manager.* "But, it's a family business, your family's store," she heard herself say, and then could have kicked herself for uttering those words. She settled for a self-inflicted pinch in the thigh underneath the table. She wanted this opportunity. She never dreamed of it though. Her only dream was one which was far from reality, and probably never would be. Edie, her sister of all people, was living that dream. In Tate's arms.

"My family," Tate paused, "is incomplete now. My Pops adored you, and so does Ma. Kathy wants no part of the market.

You know I don't either. I was just doing what I had to do. But you, Syd, are a natural in there. I mean, come on, since high school Ry's Market has been like your second home. You would have left long ago if you hated it, right?" Tate was partly correct. Sure, she felt at ease and in her element, in the job she held since she was a teenager. The root of her sustained growth there, however, stemmed from Sydney Klein's fear of those jagged edges of change. She always stayed where she was comfortable. She didn't dare venture out anywhere else. She was like that in her career of choice – and in her personal life. Sydney had a few friends in her circle, but her dating life was null. Her closest friends knew why. She wouldn't allow room in her heart for another man.

"I don't know what to say," Sydney admitted.

"Don't say anything yet," Tate told her. "Just handle what needs to be done while I'm out, and I'll talk to my mother. I do want to include her, but she's so fragile right now, and this really is my decision. It's my position and I want you to have it."

Sydney kept her hands on her lap underneath the table in front of her. They were trembling. She wasn't scared of this opportunity. She had some faith in herself. She knew it would be a perfect fit for her. *Store manager.* Tate Ryman had given her something just now. A chance. He believed in her. No one else really ever had. Not like that anyway. And Sydney could feel herself falling even harder for this man.

And just like any other time when the two of them were connecting, the kitchen door flung open from the mudroom, and in walked Edie.

Under her long winter white coat, she was dressed to the nines in flared-legged black dress pants that fit high on her narrow waistline, and a skintight lavender turtleneck sweater with a sparkly silver infinity scarf which hung around her neck and rested on her full chest. A chest she paid to have enhanced when she was old enough not to need parental consent. In her black high heels, Edie was every bit as tall as Tate when he stood up from his chair and turned to face her as she rushed through the door and into his arms. "Oh, babes, come here. I'm so, so sorry about your Pops. He was a gem, just the best man ever." Sydney all but rolled her eyes far back into her head as she remained seated in her chair at the opposite end of the table. *Yeah, if he was such a wonderful man in her eyes, why wasn't Edie there when he took his final breath today?* Sydney watched her sister wrapped up in Tate's arms. He held her close. He adored her, that much was blatantly obvious.

Edie was still touching him, rubbing his back and shoulders, and placing her hands on his chest when they pulled apart. "Syd," Edie finally acknowledged her. "I didn't see your car out front."

"It's in the shop," she stated, and Tate quickly glanced at her, realizing he had missed seeing it as well.

"You walked here? It's freezing out…"

"A friend gave me a ride," Sydney replied. Tate was touched. Sydney did not have access to a vehicle, but she had found a way to get there, to be there to support him.

"Well we do appreciate you being here, especially since I couldn't be – at a moment's notice," Edie refrained from mentioning how she was only on an early lunch break and needed to return to the office again within the hour. She spoke, touching Tate's face in Sydney's presence, and he still had an arm around her waist. That hourglass waist. Sydney had been sucking in her stomach flab the entire time she was seated at the table with Tate. She saw how his flannel shirt hugged his biceps and outlined his tight abs. Even through clothes, Sydney could tell how incredibly toned he was. Her sister, as well. It sickened her, and even still she could imagine their fit and fabulous naked bodies intertwined in the heat of sex.

"I have to go," Sydney popped up from her chair too abruptly and bumped the table, wobbling her empty coffee mug a bit.

"What about a ride?" Tate asked her, genuinely concerned about her being out in the cold. He wouldn't allow her to walk and she knew it.

"I'll call for one," she said, moving awkwardly past both of them and toward the door leading out into the mudroom. All Sydney heard after that was a meaningless *okay, thanks for coming,* from her sister. And when she looked up gracelessly at Tate, he had given her a genuine smile. She imagined he was thinking, *remember what we talked about,* as she stepped out of the door and closed it behind her.

By the time Sydney had walked to the end of the long rocked driveway, she had called for a ride. A friend was en route to pick her up. She pulled up her pink hood, and shoved her hands inside of the front pouch of the fleece sweatshirt. Tate was watching her from the window that spanned almost the entire length of the mudroom. He had stepped out there in his socks to make sure Sydney would get home safely. While she stood curbside in the frigid weather, Edie called Tate back into the house. And he obliged by walking away from the window and going inside.

Chapter 2

Tate was relieved that it was over. After two days of everything pertaining to his father's funeral, he almost felt as if he could breathe again. He would miss his father for the rest of his life, but after hearing everyone else say it to him in recent days, Tate began to believe it. *His father was in a better place.* He lived almost seventy years of a very good life. Sure, it should have been longer. And healthier his last couple of years. But, life was like that at times. *Difficult. Trying. Unpredictable.*

He sat on the bottom step in the mudroom at the entrance to his house. He had ripped up the ugly green outdoor carpet that had been there when he moved in almost six years ago, and he replaced it with prefinished hardwood. He had chosen a barnwood color flooring that looked rustic and outdoorsy. He looked down at his thick white socks planted on that wood flooring now. It was a do-it-yourself project for any man with basic carpentry skills, but for Tate it was as simple as putting a puzzle together. He missed hardcore construction, and he wished the winter would pass quickly so he could get back to it. In the coming months, his objective was to cut his ties with managing Ry's Market. And Tate knew Sydney was the answer for him to transition out of the store and back to construction. He pulled out his cell phone from the rear pocket of his faded denim, and he sent her a text.

Are you free for lunch?

Tate walked over to the window, stood there, and looked out of it. He lived away from the in-town activity where it was nothing to walk down the street and find a hybrid vehicle following a horse and buggy. It took all kinds of people to keep Camden, Delaware afloat, even the Amish community. It was a small town with great history. Beautiful old houses, like the one Tate had snagged, as well as breathtaking new homes, and everything else in between. Tate's parents had owned the only small-town grocery store in existence for over fifty years. They were the kind of people who believed in still helping their patrons carry their grocery bags to their car. And they knew them all by their first name. It was sleeting on the window as Tate stood near it. Winters were cold enough there, but temperatures seldom dropped to zero degrees. Clouds were common, and the Delaware Bay winds often caused fog. What

Tate longed for and needed right now was sunlight. His wish was for it to be mid or late April when he could get back outside and build something. He retrieved his phone again from his pocket to be sure Sydney had not responded. The volume was maximized, and there were no new messages. She was going to be his ticket to moving on with his life. He needed her.

Sydney Klein sat in the cramped office at Ry's Market. There was just enough room in there to fill the space of a walk-in closet, but instead there was a small metal desk and an old worn black leather swivel chair. The only thing not outdated in there was the laptop computer that Sydney was working on.

It had been five days since Tate asked her to fill his shoes at his family's market. At first, it felt awfully strange to walk into that cramped office and not be in there to punch her time card, request a day off, or to have something work-related to discuss with someone else who was in charge. Sydney had been on the receiving end of looks at the market from her coworkers, and more than a few questions about *why she was in there,* and *what was she doing all day, and who was going to fill her spot at the register?* It stressed her and made her feel frazzled as she unwrapped another Kraft caramel cube from its clear plastic wrapper and chewed while she punched the keys on the keypad in front of her. She always consumed more junk food when she felt stressed out. This morning she was ordering groceries, and later she would do the employee payroll. Sydney had just swallowed the piece of candy and was going for another when the office door opened behind her. And when she turned and saw Tate walk in and close the door, she no longer wanted that fifth piece of caramel in her hand.

"Hiya Syd," he said, strolling in as if he owned the place. And, well, he did.

"Um, hi," she never could hide the nervous jitter in her voice when she was around him. "I can get up, um, and go, if you need to-" As Sydney started to stand up, her white tennis shoes squeaked on the waxed green and white tiled floor. Tate placed his hands on both of her shoulders, on the Ry's Market burgundy smock she was wearing, and he settled her back down on the chair.

"Sit. No getting up and running out of here just because I'm in the building. This is your job now, Syd. Own it." Tate had not officially told his mother, but for Sydney the position was as good as hers regardless.

Tate sat down on the desktop directly in front of Sydney. There was no other place to sit, not unless he had wanted to drag the metal chair out of the corner where it was folded and propped against the wall.

Sydney's first instinct was to roll her chair back, to put some space between his legs and hers. But then, when she thought about it -when she really focused on how close he was to her- she stayed put. Tate could see she was staring, but her eye contact ceased when he caught her. He looked down at her jeans and her full thighs. She had been bending her toes upward on the floor to keep those thighs from flattening on the chair. She was a little on the chubby side, but Tate thought of her as a cute kid sister. She was, after all, his girlfriend's next of kin.

"I texted you awhile ago," he said, as he watched her cheeks flush.

"My phone, it's in my purse in my locker," those lockers were on the short wall in that same room, just opposite from where she sat now, "and probably not even powered on," she told him, and he shook his head, smiling.

"Rule number one, if you are going to be store manager," he began, and she nodded before he even finished his statement. "Keep your damn phone on, and with you. Your number is going to be the point of contact for business here. Got it?"

"Okay, sorry," Sydney told him.

"No need to apologize," he tried getting her to relax. He knew it was a feat that was possible. He had seen her calm and cool before. He actually believed she could be fun. What he liked most about her was that she was real. What you saw with Sydney Klein was precisely what you got. She cared more about people's feelings than she did about fashion. She would rather over tip a waiter than waste any money on makeup or a manicure. She was every bit as low maintenance as her big sister was high maintenance. "But, you did miss a really important text from me earlier," he added.

"Should I get my phone?" Sydney asked, attempting to rise off of that chair again, but Tate stopped her.

RECKLESS

"I'll relay the message for you," he spoke, and then broke into a silly smile. "Are you free for lunch?"

"Me?" she felt flustered. "You want to have lunch with me? But, I have an order to place, and payroll to complete, and–"

"Slow down sister, that can all wait," Tate said, and she could have frowned to express her disappointment. The last thing she wanted was for Tate Ryman to think of her as *his sister*. Before she made another attempt to stand up, he rolled back her chair with her still on it. He also closed the laptop on the desk so she would stop looking past him and at it. "It will be a business lunch. Come on…" He pulled her up to her feet in those white tennis shoes with the thick rubber soles. Her hands felt cold and clammy in his, but that only made him smile. *Her quirks were cute.*

Tate cleared his plate from the dinner table, and walked up to the kitchen sink. When he turned around to retrieve his empty milk glass from the table, he heard Edie's car coming up the driveway. A minute or two later, once she made her way from the detached garage, Edie walked in through the mud-room and up those few steps into the kitchen.

"Oh," Edie looked regretful as she took off her long winter white coat and folded it over one of the kitchen chairs. "I'm so sorry I'm late, but I had hoped you would wait."

"It's seven o'clock, E," he told her. "I was hungry, and besides you never said you were on your way or anything. I only ate a grilled cheese, I can make you one if you'd like?"

Edie looked at him and rolled her eyes. "You know I don't eat like that. I'll tear up some lettuce for a salad later," she said, opening the refrigerator to eye up a head of lettuce in the bottom produce drawer. And then she took out an already open bottle of white wine and poured herself a generous glass on the countertop.

Her days were long as an advertising executive at a firm in Dover, less than ten minutes of drive time away. She loved her job, she craved success and money, and she attained it by working too much.

"How was your day?" he asked her, bracing himself to hear all about the clients and accounts that he cared nothing for.

"Crazy busy," she said, not making an effort to ask him how his day was, or how he had spent it. She assumed he went back to work at the market since the cold winter weather would keep him away from construction for a few more months. Edie did know Tate had no intention of running his parents' market for the rest of his life. And, for that, she was relieved. She was embarrassed to say her boyfriend managed a grocery store. She believed it was much more socially acceptable to say he was in construction. Edie was aware that Tate had moved Sydney up the ladder at Ry's Market. She actually giggled when he told her, still believing her little sister was going nowhere in life.

"But, let's not talk about work. In fact," she said, "let's not talk at all."

Tate could taste the wine on her lips and on her tongue as she kissed him hard and full on the mouth, standing in front of their kitchen sink. He kissed her back. *What man wouldn't desire a woman like Edie Klein?* When she had him wanting more, Edie stepped back and took a hold of the tiny gold zipper placed slightly above her cleavage on her black dress. She pulled it down until her dress split in two where it ended just above her knees. The dress dropped to the tile floor and she stood there in her matching black bra, black thong, and the two-inch black high heels that put her eye to eye with her man. Her man that stared at her right now with sheer desire in his eyes. He put his hands on her bare, full, shapely rear, and pulled her close. He kissed her hard as he slipped his fingers in the front of her panties. It was only a few minutes after seven o'clock, and he was certain he was already going to lay her down on their bed. That was how they compensated for a lack of communication in their relationship. And, so far, that had been enough.

Chapter 3

When Tate told his mother of his plans for Ry's Market, she cried. She sat in one of the two ivory-colored comfortable chairs that bookended the matching sofa in her living room. Her hands were on her lap. She was dressed cozy in a pale pink fleece sweatsuit with tan moccasin slippers on her stocking feet. Tate had knelt down beside her, the knees of his worn jeans on the burgundy berber carpet, and he covered both of her hands with one of his. She seemed so small, so frail. Gone were the years when Tate recalled her taking him by the hand, making him feel safe and loved, and simply wanting her to lead the way. He felt tremendous guilt at this moment for letting his mother down. But, the market was not for him. Not for the rest of his life.

"Ma…I'm really sorry. I promise you, the market will be in the best hands," Tate tried to reassure her, as he watched her pull out a wadded up tissue from her pants pocket and she dabbed her eyes and then her nose with what was left of it. Her white hair was cut into a bob that ended at her earlobes, as Tate always remembered. It was once as sandy brown as Tate's hair. He had his mother's blue eyes, too.

"I don't want you bringing in a stranger, no big wigs in our little market. He won't fit in here, not in our small town, and not in our store. Your father would–"

"Ma, please…" Tate interrupted her, and he tried to do so politely. "You know me better than that, don't you? Syd has already proven she can carry us."

"Excuse me? Little Miss Sydney, who hasn't left the register adjacent to aisle three since she was sixteen?" Mary Lou Ryman scoffed and made a huffing sound. It was an old woman's way of disapproving.

"Ma, you've always cared about her. Don't knock her. She is shy, I know, but she has welcomed this change with open arms. She truly is a very smart girl. You just have to get to know her." Tate was trying, in Syd's defense, but he also was speaking the truth.

"I've known her for ten years, and yes she seems sweet and all good," Mary Lou spoke, and nodded her head in agreement with her only son. *But, could she manage a store? Their market?*

"So what's the problem then? She's the next best thing to running the market than me, right?" Tate awaited his mother's answer.

"No, that would be Kathy, but we both know hell freezing over is more likely to happen before your sister would ever even consider such a thing." Mary Lou grinned.

"You see, there ya go! You still love Kathy and she never wanted to work a day in our store. I now have faith that you will not disown me for this decision." Tate smiled wide at his mother, as he was still bent on his knees in front of her.

"Nothing you could ever do would make me stop loving you, my boy," she told him. "I will trust you have made a good decision."

Tate leaned forward and his mother wrapped her arms around his neck as he kissed her in between the wrinkle folds on her cheek. "I know I have. Thank you, Ma."

All Mary Lou had ever wanted for her children was not unlike every other mother out there. She wanted them to be happy, in their careers and in their personal lives. She was old school, yes, and she had wished for her son to be married to the woman he was *shacked up with*. Not that Mary Lou was especially fond of the Barbie doll her son was in love with. Edie Klein was superficial and hardly maternal which crushed any hope Mary Lou had of becoming a grandmother again. But, that was an opinion she had only voiced to her husband when he was alive. He used to just chuckle and remind his wife that their son was a young man and only had one thing on his mind. And Mary Lou had hoped and prayed with her rosary every night for that to be true. *Her son was young. Maybe he would outgrow that woman.*

The text that Tate received from Edie read: *I'm working late tonight.* After two years together, Tate was beginning to grow tired of it. *Eating dinner alone. Sharing small talk, but never really embracing conversation.* Everything about his life right now felt as if it was hanging in the balance. *He was missing his father. He wanted to walk away from the family business, once and for all.* And he needed to talk about it with someone.

Tate threw on his brown thermal-lined coat with a warm hood that he often wore when he went hunting. He put his gloveless hands into his pockets, left his house, and began to walk the length of his driveway. He didn't know where he was going, he only knew he needed to clear his head. After pacing the long rock driveway twice, back and forth in the cold wind, Tate ended up in the detached garage, inside of his truck. He started the engine, backed all the way down the lane road, and then he drove into town.

Adjacent to Ry's Market was Lantern Inn. It was the bar, downtown, where Tate first saw Edie. She caught his eye like no other woman had. She had stolen his heart. He used to believe there was no way he could ever let her go. They shared this electricity, this magnetic attraction that was once so powerful. They certainly weren't boring. But in the last several months, there was some distance emotionally that had not been there before. It was beginning to happen, and Tate had yet to grasp it. Lovers, no longer blinded by beauty and lust, often become intense in a new way as they truly get to know each other. Tate was beginning to question whether or not they could make their relationship work. Maybe he was ready to settle down. Children, no children, possibly he was ready, possibly she was not. Marriage should come first, especially in a small town like Camden. Those were conversations the two of them needed to have together. Edie was a very complex woman. And Tate felt deeply connected to her. *But, was he staying in their relationship for all the wrong reasons?*

His Timberland work boots on the sticky barroom floor felt oddly familiar in a comfortable sense as Tate walked up to the near-empty bar. Lantern Inn used to serve as a hotel upstairs, but that was no more. Now, the owner of the bar occupied that space with his own living quarters. Tate sat down on a stool at the end, just a few bar stools away from a town drunk everyone knew as Rudi. Rudi meant no harm. He was in his sixties now, and it had been twenty years since he lost his family. His wife and both of his children perished in a house fire. Life had amounted to getting drunk every night at Lantern Inn for Rudi. And most people in that town, who had ever loved and lost a spouse or a child, didn't blame him. Or judge him.

Tate nodded at Rudi and said, *Hey man, how ya doing.* Rudi lifted his eyes from his longneck and looked over at Tate, but he never responded.

"What'll it be?" Bartender Jack asked Tate a moment after he sat down on the cushioned red stool with a significant tear on the side and no backing.

"Bud Light on draft, Jack, thanks." Tate had known Jack since high school. He had let himself go. Beer belly. Always unshaven. And a long, greasy ponytail that reached halfway down his back. He had a story, too. The tattoo on his left forearm of the twin towers with a cross intertwined between them told of his tragedy. His father was a fireman who was killed in the 9-11 attacks on the World Trade Center. His mother lost her mind in the years that followed, and she was now locked up in a mental institution. Jack stopped visiting her when he began to grow into a man. The site of him had sent his mother into hysterics each time. She couldn't take even looking at him, as his resemblance to his father was strong. Jack had tried to move on, to make a life of his own. And then the girl he wanted to marry had hung herself in their bedroom. Life was cruel and heartless sometimes. That was why Tate never judged. Everyone had a story, and some were too heartbreaking to talk about. Bartending and sleeping with any woman who ended up too drunk to drive home had become a way of life for Jack. *At least he was getting laid*, Tate thought, smirking to himself. *A man's gotta get some enjoyment out of a crummy life.*

After his third beer, it was only Tate and Jack left in the bar. Tate hadn't remembered it ever being so slow in there before when he used to stop in a few nights a week. "Where is everybody tonight?" Tate finally asked Jack when he finished wiping down the bar, beginning on the far end and finishing next to Tate's beer glass. The rag he used reeked of something sour, and Tate backed up on his stool when his sense of smell overwhelmed him.

"I was wondering the same," Jack responded. "Not a woman in sight in here tonight! What the fuck is it? Do I smell?"

Something sure as hell does, Jack felt like saying, but he refrained. "Well damn the luck for you tonight, pal," Tate teased him, and Jack shook his head in sheer disappointment.

"What are you doing in here anyways? Having a woman with a body like Edie Klein's, you should be at home taking your time on her."

"Hey now," Tate didn't want to hear another man talk about her like that. But, he knew they all did. *They were men. And Edie was indeed beautiful and sexy.* "She's working late."

"Ah, I see," Jack nodded. "Are you sure that's not just an excuse?"

"Absolutely I'm sure," Tate told him, adamantly.

"Then what's troubling you. I know your Pops met his maker..."

"I won't cry in my beer in front of you. You've had your share." Tate was referring to Jack losing his father when he was just fifteen years old and how that was only the beginning of his losses.

"How considerate of you. Not too many folks think twice before they complain. Yeah, I know pain," Jack agreed, taking Tate's glass and refilling it from the tap. He also filled a second glass for himself as he remained standing directly across the bar from Tate. "Are you a happy man?" Jack asked Tate, assuming so. He had a business to run, a remodeled home with generous land on the outskirts of town, and a picture-perfect woman. Jack actually felt jealous. All he had was a bar.

"I am," Tate answered. "Just feeling a little lost at the moment." Jack rested his elbows on top of the bar, and there was something in his eyes that encouraged Tate to feel like he could talk to him. They had never been remotely close, but they were friendly in passing. *What would it hurt to tell this guy a little bit of what was weighing on him?* Besides, on his fourth beer, Tate had a pretty good buzz going on. "I'm leaving the market for good, I can't bring myself to be like my Pops. I'm going back to construction."

"Nothing wrong with that at all," Jack stated.

"No, just a disappointed Ma, but she'll come around. She has no other choice," Tate told him. "And then there's Edie. The sex is good..." Jack groaned from behind the bar. Tate wasn't sure if he wanted to be spared the details or not. "But, we've reached a crossroad."

"Oh for chrissakes Ryman, just give her a ring. All women want to make it official." Jack was serious, and Tate looked at him as if he had just slapped some sense into him.

"So you think that's it? You think she could be feeling the same as I am? We just need to kick things up a notch and get married? Get serious? Maybe have babies?" Tate suddenly felt as if that was the answer. Edie needed a solid commitment from him. She was an independent woman, possibly too proud to confront him on the subject of commitment. She had never even dropped a single hint. They just didn't talk about the future.

It was well past business hours, and Edie was still behind her desk on the ninth floor of Stockmann Advertising. As an account executive, Edie provided a link between clients and the agency. She was responsible for coordinating advertising campaigns. Communication was the key to the success of her position, and Edie had spent years proving she had analytical, organizing, leadership, interpersonal, oral and written communication skills. Her strengths in each of those only continued to become more impressive. Edie understood how businesses work and how they profit. She was hardly a lightweight and the executives at Stockmann Advertising saw Edie Klein as a huge benefit to their clients and their firm. She was a keeper.

That was the professional side of Edie. The personal side almost altogether the opposite. Edie expected her friends and her family to be there for her when she needed them. And they were. It was Edie who was rarely present for anyone – unless she benefited from it somehow. Edie was reckless with relationships and she was the last person to ever recognize that fact. She defined self-centered. But, she was envied – regardless. Edie shined. It was as if a light followed her everywhere. And everyone who stood beside her, paled in comparison. Her sister felt threatened and belittled by that feeling with Edie. And Tate had the woman he was in love with placed so high up on a pedestal that he didn't want to see it. He still caught himself wondering why she ever chose him. Edie Klein had given him a confidence he never carried before – because she wanted him.

It was almost nine o'clock before Edie realized it was getting late, and she needed to go home. She had not received a response from Tate after she texted him four hours ago. She assumed he was miffed because she had not been home in time for dinner again. He would get over it though. He always did.

She powered off her computer and stood up from behind her desk. Her long winter white coat felt cozy when she slipped it on and fastened it close to her body. The furnace didn't run as much in the building, on the ninth floor, at nighttime.

There were only two other cars in the dim-lit parking lot when Edie got into hers. She could hardly wait turn on the heat when she started the engine and began to defrost the windshield. The air coming through the vents was cold, and Edie felt chilled as it blasted directly on her face. She just wanted to go home, and be warm.

The fog was thick as she drove, but she had ventured those roads too many times to count, day and night, to let the weather conditions alarm her. Her radio was turned up loud and the pointed-toe of her black heel was holding steady on the gas pedal. She was watching the road diligently, looking for the tail lights of a possible vehicle in front of her, but it appeared as if it was just her and the heavy fog out there on that long stretch of road.

She never saw it coming. Until its bright headlights were right in front of her. Edie was in her lane, centered exactly where she was supposed to be. It was the driver of the full-size pickup truck that apparently crossed over the center line when the fog blurred his vision and he lost his bearings. He had been driving on the wrong side of the road. Edie saw the truck, and she immediately swerved to the right and veered her car off of the road at the last possible second.

Chapter 4

There was no impact. Or at least, Edie didn't think there was. Her car hit the ditch so fast and with an incredible force. The airbag in front of her did not function in time to protect Edie from slamming her forehead into the steering wheel. The force threw her back and against the driver's seat. And then her body went limp.

She had no concept of how much time had passed, but the next thing Edie knew, she was able to open the car door, and step out into the dark, cold night. She saw that pickup truck, undamaged and now parked on the side of the road, and assumed it was the driver who was talking to either a police officer or paramedic. It was too dark for her to differentiate.

Edie called out to them, but her words went unheard. She started to step closer, to climb the ditch with her pointed-toe black heels firmly on the ground. She almost made it into the stream of headlights on the road. But then, she stopped. She instantly froze when she saw a man walking toward her. Her eyes had to be failing her. She had hit her head, she remembered, but it didn't hurt. She felt absolutely no pain. She didn't even feel cold right now in the winter's night air. And she always felt cold. Tate teased her time and again because of all the layers she wore during the overcast Camden winters. The man she saw approached her, but he waited for Edie to speak first.

She did not move. And she stared. "No? It can't be. You're-" Edie wanted to say *dead* but the word never came. Because Tate's father looked real, and very much alive to her right now. "Mr. Ryman? What is happening here?"

Edie watched Tate's father look past her and over at her car, positioned nose down in the ditch. Edie turned around swiftly and what she saw alarmed her beyond words. The paramedics were frantically working. She –her body– was still in the car and was now being taken out of it, carefully but quickly. Her body was lifted, carried, and placed on top of a stretcher that belonged in an ambulance or a hospital. She could see her own body that this was happening to. *But, she was fine.*

She was right here. Standing beside Mr.–

"Oh dear God! I'm dead! You're here and I can see you and I'm now where you are. NO!" Edie screamed and Mr. Ryman took two steps toward her.

"You're not dead…" She heard his words. He was speaking to her. *But she wasn't as dead as he was?*

Edie intently studied Mr. Ryman. She had not seen him look remotely as healthy in a very long time. His eyes were bright. His gray hair was full and wavy. He looked good again. His jeans and tucked-in flannel shirt with brown-tie shoes all looked so real. *But he wasn't real. What was happening could not be possible.*

She started to stumble away from him, toward the scene. But, he prevented her. "No, Edie. You must stay with me for awhile."

Edie spoke adamantly as fear surfaced in her voice and was clearly expressed on her face. "Tell me what is going on!"

"You were in a car accident, and I've been sent to help you figure out a few things before you return to that body you are looking at over there." Mr. Ryman's voice was calm. So calm that it had almost put Edie at ease. But this situation was forcing her to panic a little bit more with each passing second.

"So, I'm going to be okay?" Edie needed reassurance. She instantly called him out on what he had just told her. *Before you return to your body.* "I mean, this is some kind of crazy, I don't know what, that is happening to me right now, but I will live. I will live, right?"

"Let's take a walk, get away from this scene for awhile…" Mr. Ryman suggested and Edie felt as if she had no other choice. She stood there for a moment and watched him begin to walk away from her. She unfastened her long winter white coat, draped it over her arm. It just didn't feel all that cold out there. And then she had to sprint in her heels to catch up to him.

※

Tate rushed through the emergency room doors at Bayhealth Medical Center. He had arrived home minutes ago. He also drove in the heavy fog that was the worst he remembered it being in years. Then a uniformed police officer knocked on his front door. *There was a car accident, Edie ran her vehicle off of the road, and was taken by ambulance to Bayhealth.*

He was told to have a seat and wait. Tate didn't know if he should call Sydney. She was the only family Edie had left. He was hoping this wasn't that dire. He didn't know anything about Edie's condition yet, and that was making him crazy. He needed her. He loved her. He was sitting there with an engagement ring in the front pocket of his jeans. It was a two and a half carat pear-shaped diamond in a little black velvet box. He had left the bar and walked two blocks down to Camden's only jewelry store. It had cost him a small fortune, but this wasn't just for any woman. It had to be exquisite and fitting for only Edie. He wanted the best diamond for her, and Tate believed he had found it. He now wanted a chance to give this ring to Edie. To see it on her finger. To watch her facial expression when he proposed. To feel her lips on his after she said *yes. They had a life to plan and carry out together. Why was this happening now? And what exactly happened to Edie?*

The waiting room was chaotic, and Tate found an empty chair in the center. He sat there with his body bent forward. He ran his fingers through his unruly hair. His sandy brown locks were winged around his ears, forehead, and the back of his neck. He knew he reeked of bar smell. Smoke and booze. He just stared at the floor, and he had no idea how much time had passed before he heard Edie's name. *Who's here for Miss Edie Klein?*

Tate stood up from his chair so abruptly that he pushed it backward and it made a loud squeaking sound on the vinyl tile flooring. "I'm here for Edie," he said, trying not to appear panicked. But he was. He feared what would happen next.

The doctor had a full head of gray hair, and Tate thought he looked old enough to be his father. For a moment, he wanted to dwell on the ache he felt from having just lost him. The doctor led Tate down a long hallway and stopped in front of a closed door of a patient room. As they walked, Tate was trying to process everything he had told him. *Edie suffered a harsh blow to her forehead. She had moderate inflammation, and minimal bleeding from her nose and ears.* As the doctor stopped walking, Tate did as well.

"I've ruled out any internal bleeding at this point," the physician said.

"So I can see her now? Is this her room?" Tate suddenly

felt optimistic. *Edie hit her head and was a little banged up but she would pull through.*

"Yes, this is her room. She's not awake yet, though. She's unconscious but stable. We have not ruled out a concussion, but her pupils are not dilated and her eyes are not bloodshot. All good signs," the doctor concluded.

"So she just has to wake up then," Tate added, cautiously.

"Yes," the doctor replied, as he pushed open the door and Tate followed him inside.

There was a vacant hospital bed, and next to it was the bed Edie was lying on. A dim light shown above the empty bed, but it was dark on Edie's side of the room. Tate followed, slowly, into the room. Before he even reached her bedside, he felt as if he needed a moment to regain his composure. To get his emotions in check. To him, Edie was always incredibly together. Flawless. The times were rare when he didn't see makeup applied to perfection on her face and eyes. Those ironically were the times he had loved her most. When she was bare-boned, natural, and real. This was different though. This was frightening. She almost looked…lifeless.

When Tate did reach her bedside, he wanted to touch her hand. He started to reach for it, bending slightly over the bed, until he gave in and sat down on the chair beside it to be closer to her. The doctor was watching him, but Tate only had his eyes on Edie. The thick bandage across her forehead. A few scratches on her face. He could hear her complaining now about the injury…the scar, the imperfection. *It could have been so much worse,* Tate thought to himself, as he stared at her long, blonde hair, her full eyelashes that were fanned out just above her cheek bones.

"It's good to talk to patients who are comatose. She can hear you," the doctor offered.

"So that's what this is? Edie is in a coma? For how long?" Tate asked, sounding like a child with fear in his voice.

"That we do not know. It's puzzling to see her under this long actually. She's breathing on her own. Her injury doesn't quite match up to the brain's need to rest to this extent. I suspect she will wake up soon." Tate wasn't really listening to the doctor's words that followed, because he had started to speak to Edie as if they were the only two present in that sterile hospital room. And he had not noticed when the doctor quietly slipped out of the room.

They never walked through the parking lot or entered the door. Mr. Ryman and Edie were just suddenly inside of Ry's Market. It was late at night, and the store had been closed for hours. Edie wanted to ask him what they were doing there, but then she thought about where they were and what this place had meant to Rex Ryman for almost his entire life. She wondered then if he came there frequently. If he was *among* the shoppers at any given moment. That idea both freaked her and fascinated her. When she returned to her life –her real life, not this ghost-like limbo– Edie wanted to tell her sister about this. Exactly what she cannot see happening around her while she was working. Edie smiled to herself. She knew Sydney would flip out. And it was as if she had always gotten some form of enjoyment out of her little sister being unsettled or upset.

Finally, as they approached what Edie saw was the office in that building, she asked Mr. Ryman what they were doing there. "Is there a reason you have brought me here?" she spoke, as he stopped in front of the faux dark wood door that read OFFICE.

"There's going to be a reason for our stops on this journey. I am not your source for answers. You can gather all you need just by watching." As Mr. Ryman spoke, Edie felt confused and even a little miffed. He was purposely being vague. She didn't have time to take part in any journey. She just wanted to get back to her life. She left work behind at the office tonight that she needed to tend to first thing in the morning. The only reason she had not completed it was she had to get home to Tate. She drove home in the dense fog to be with him.

Edie's black pointed-toe heels were now on the waxed floor on the opposite side of the door. There, she saw Sydney burning the midnight oil. She was surprised to see her sister working at a computer. The room was small. The furniture was even older than Sydney's burgundy Ry's Market smock. But, as Edie judged all of her surroundings, she found herself studying her sister. A part of her wished she could say, *Hey Syd, I'm here*, but spying felt more interesting at the moment. Mr. Ryman had told her to observe and learn. Edie was about to try.

She stepped closer, directly behind her sister. Just then, Sydney stretched her arms up high above her head, overtop the chair and into the air. Edie was taken aback that those arms had not hit her. She was right there and that force had gone directly through her body. As if she wasn't really there. Mr. Ryman chuckled and Edie turned to him with wide eyes. "You've had some time to get used to that. I haven't! You're sure I'm not ...you know...dead?" Mr. Ryman brought a finger to his lips as if to shush her, and then he pointed over at Sydney with that same finger. Edie comprehended the message. She was supposed to be watching, listening, and learning.

The only thing Edie could gather from this scene was her sister sitting there, working on what appeared to be payroll. *So what? She was working overtime to ensure every employee under that old rickety roof would receive a direct deposit first thing in the morning when the bank opened. She felt like rolling her eyes at the important career her sister believed she had. The same job since she was a teenager.*

Edie wondered now if Mr. Ryman could read her mind. Had he known she was thinking such demeaning thoughts? Anything could be possible, considering where they were and how they currently *existed.* She hoped that Tate's father didn't know what she was thinking. She assumed he had always liked her because of how he had welcomed her into Tate's life and their family with such grace.

Sydney's cell phone rang. Edie watched her pick it up to answer. She could easily hear Tate's voice on the opposite end. "Syd...I'm sorry to wake you."

"You didn't. I'm at the market, working late. Payroll is due." Edie could see her sister's face flush as she walked around and sat on the edge of the desk in front of her. Edie was so close to her sister right now, and again Sydney was oblivious.

"I'm calling with some… I have some not-so-good news. It's bad, but it's going to get better. It has to." Tate was rambling and Sydney looked up and frowned. It was almost as if she had seen Edie sitting there, because her eyes were focused on her. For a moment anyway, Edie felt as if Sydney could see her. But, there was no possible way. "Edie was in an accident tonight. I'm at Bayhealth with her now."

"An accident? What kind? Was she hurt?" Sydney remained seated in her chair, and surprisingly Edie thought she looked unfazed. And that would be unbelievable because it never took much to frazzle her sister.

"She ran her car off the road. She hit her head pretty hard. And, right now, she's still unconscious." Tate tried to explain the news slowly as he expected it would alarm Sydney.

"Oh my God… I'll be there soon." Sydney ended their phone call and sat there for a moment. Edie watched her take the time to close out of the computer program and power off the machine. She didn't rush. She didn't curse or talk aloud to herself as many people did in an emergency situation when they could hardly think straight in a rush. But, Sydney took the time to shut the office down, lights and all, before she slowly and calmly walked out of the building. Edie never even looked to see if Mr. Ryman was following her, she only thought for a split second that she needed go after her sister. And then, instantly, Edie and Mr. Ryman were in the parking lot. They were watching Sydney stroll to her car. Again, she was in no panic, no rush.

There was a full-size pickup truck out there with its lights on, parked nose to nose with Sydney's compact car. Sydney stood outside of that truck and so did its male driver. Edie moved closer so she could hear their conversation.

Edie didn't recognize the man, who appeared to be about her sister's age, as he spoke first. "I did what you asked. I know it's not the outcome you expected." The man lit up a cigarette as he spoke to Sydney in the parking lot where only two pole lights above them lit the area.

"We don't know the outcome. You will not get paid until *it* happens." Sydney's voice was strong and her eyes looked angry. Edie did not recognize her own sister.

"What the fuck?" the man, who now looked shady to Edie, exclaimed. "We had an agreement for me to run your sister off the road. What happened after that was out of my control! You owe me, bitch!"

"Half," Sydney spoke up, and little did she know that Edie was right there, close by and towering over her. Edie had wide eyes, an open mouth, and she was listening so intently in a state of sheer shock. "You will get half now, and the rest when my sister dies."

Chapter 5

Tate dozed off at Edie's bedside. He was not awake when her eyes twitched and her facial expression tensed. What Edie was experiencing while she was under had been affecting her as she lied there in that hospital bed. Her physical being was now in a frantic hurry to wake up. But it wasn't time yet.

He was unsure how long he had been sitting there with his eyes closed in the chair near Edie's hospital bedside, but Tate was startled awake when he felt someone gently touch his shoulder.

"Syd, hi," Tate said, shifting his body weight in the uncomfortable chair.

"I can't believe this is happening," Sydney said, looking at her sister lying there, unconscious, and banged up. "What did the doctor say? I mean, when will she wake up?"

"Soon," Tate said, trying to sound positive. He had not expected this reaction from Edie's little sister. She was prone to fall apart. Sydney stood closer to the bedside and Tate noticed she was still wearing her burgundy Ry's Market smock. She had suddenly turned into a workaholic – just like her sister. If Edie had not been so hell-bent on working late hours, the accident never would have happened. She would not be lying in that hospital bed now.

"I'm just expecting her to wake up and talk snarky to me, you know?" Sydney said, looking over at Tate and then back at Edie. "It feels strange to see her like this. So helpless."

"I know what you mean," Tate said, as he focused his worried eyes on Edie. "She's just always so together. So beautiful. This isn't her."

Sydney tensed, but hid her emotions well. *You are the one who needs to wake up, Tate Ryman. Can't you see? She is not the woman for you. And she never will be. You're going to realize that sooner or later. I'll help you come to your senses.*

"Thanks for coming here," Tate added.

"Of course," Sydney told him. "I wouldn't be anywhere else. My sister needs me." Tate reached for Sydney's hand and he held it. Her face didn't flush this time. She didn't feel like a nervous school girl around him. He was touching her. *It was happening already.*

Just weeks ago, Sydney had found herself staring at the laptop computer screen in that cramped office at Ry's Market. She had access to the books. The numbers were right in front of her eyes. Years of profit at the only market in the City of Camden. Sydney's paycheck was comfortable. For her. For how she was used to living. She rented a decent apartment, owned a compact hybrid, and had a little money left over to spend or save. She would never come close to seeing a six-figure salary like her sister, but for Sydney that had not been important. Even knowing that Ry's Market consistently profited around two million dollars annually for at least the last decade didn't make Sydney feel envious or greedy. She didn't want their money. She needed it to carry out her plan. Her dream to be happy.

But, how could she steal from the family who had taken care of her for so many years? They were the Rymans. It was Tate, for God's sake. Her hatred for her sister, and obsession with Tate had consumed her, and blinded her. She lost her sense of right from wrong. Sydney had spent years never getting what she wanted. Always feeling like she was lost in her sister's shadow. She wanted that to change. She wanted her sister gone. With Edie out of the picture, Sydney believed Tate would be hers.

Sydney heard of a man who lived in Dover. He had a reputation. He would do anything for a little money. After following him one night, she waited in her car outside of Lantern Inn. When he left the bar and was walking through the back ally, Sydney had approached him. It was pitch dark and her heart was about to beat through her chest. She was not *that kind of girl*. She steered clear of danger. But, her emotions had taken over. She now had the money, so she wanted the job done. And after transferring fifty thousand dollars to her personal account from the Ry's Market account, Sydney suddenly felt powerful.

Sydney told the hitman what she wanted done. He never flinched at the idea of committing a crime. He only demanded more money than he ever asked of anyone before. Considering this was murder, he expected to make some real money. His price tag was one hundred thousand dollars. Sydney was flabbergasted, and she balked, and then told him she didn't have that kind of money. He opted to settle for half. And then the two of them made a deal.

Sydney was looking at her sister in that hospital bed now. It alarmed her to think that the truth could come out. *She could go to jail. She would lose Tate.* There was no possible way that she would allow Edie to ruin her life. Not anymore than Sydney already believed she had.

Mr. Ryman stood in the parking lot while Edie nearly ran circles around him. Her heels were hitting hard on the concrete surface as she tried to escape and then paced to no avail. "Why are you just standing there? And how come we cannot follow her? She tried to have me killed! My own sister! This has to be a nightmare that I am going to wake up from any minute…"

"Edie," Mr. Ryman calmly spoke in the cold dark winter air, but neither one of them were affected by it, as they both were without coats. "You are here to fill in the blanks yourself. Come, it's time to see more."

Moments later, Edie and Mr. Ryman were inside of the home Edie remembered from her childhood. The Kleins were a blue collar family. Their father worked as an auto mechanic and their mother was a waitress at a diner in downtown Camden. They were a happy family of four, Edie remembered. The house was quiet now as Edie walked through it, her heels pressing into the shag carpet. It was as if she knew exactly where she was headed. And Mr. Ryman followed her.

In one of the back bedrooms of the house, Edie stood in the doorway watching herself at fourteen years old and Sydney was eleven. Edie's hair was long and blonde then, too. Sydney's auburn wavy locks were shoulder length then and now. Edie saw her little sister watching her apply makeup in front of a mirror attached to a dresser. She tipped a bottle of liquid foundation heavily onto her fingertips. She smeared it all over her face. It was too thick and uneven in spots.

"That looks like too much," Edie heard her little sister say to her, and before she heard herself reply, Edie already knew what she had said. She remembered those words all too clearly.

"It is too much," the fourteen-year-old Edie replied. "It's a way to cover up the pain. You should do the same."

"But, I'm too young for makeup. Mama said–"

"There's no mama anymore. It's just us, kid. And we can do whatever we want to do. Aunt Janet couldn't care less. She's only here because her name was in mama and daddy's will." Sydney listened intently to her big sister. "So, as I was saying, cover up your pain any which way. Just don't speak of it to me. I am going to be happy."

Edie stood in the doorway watching herself. She looked at Mr. Ryman as he was beside her, observing the scene from the past as well. Edie was confused about why they were there and what that meant.

"What about me?" the eleven-year-old Sydney had spoken with an innocence that should have captured Edie's attention then.

"You're on your own if you don't want to follow my lead," Edie had told her then. "No tears. No talk of our old life with them. They are gone."

"I hate makeup," Sydney responded, with tears welling up in her eyes, "and I hate you!"

Edie took a step back from the doorway, and Mr. Ryman followed.

"So you two have never been close?" he asked her, and Edie should not have been taken aback by his observation, but she was.

"Before the accident we were, I suppose, but that was a long time ago," Edie responded. "Can you at least tell me why I had to watch that just now? Is this some higher power's way of telling me it's my fault that my sister tried to kill me tonight because I wasn't there for her when our parents died?"

Edie and Sydney had been in the backseat of their family's Ford Mercury when their car was struck by another vehicle which had run a red light at an intersection. The girls walked away with only scratches, and no parents. Mr. and Mrs. Klein were killed on impact. Neither wore seatbelts, and both were thrown from the front bench seat of the car.

From that tragic day forward, Edie made a choice. Love meant pain. She would choose superficial beauty, money, prestige, and success over risking her heart pain ever again.

"These are your answers, Edie," Mr. Ryman told her. "I don't know if it will be enough, but you have to go back and try." Edie was unsure of what he meant by *try*.

Chapter 6

Edie was hurt and angry, and still engulfed in disbelief about all of this. She wanted to confront her sister. But, first, she had to wake up. She was now back inside of her body, lying in a sterile hospital bed where she was hooked up to an IV that was dripping fluids into her body, and a beeping machine was monitoring her heart rate. She had been asleep for forty-eight hours.

Tate watched her eyelids flutter. He had seen this more than a few times the past two days. He learned not to call for the nurse after the first two times. *It could be involuntary*, he was told. But, each time, Tate wanted to believe Edie was coming back to him. Each time he saw her eyelids move, he prayed that she would wake up. He had not left her side for more than hour each day to go home, take a shower, and change his clothes. During that time, he had asked Sydney to sit beside Edie so she would not be alone.

He rolled up the sleeves on his blue flannel shirt, and pushed his chair closer to her bed. He held her hand in both of his and he continued to talk to her. "E, come on. You can do it today. Open your eyes. Open them. I'm here. I'm right here. And I think you know by now that I'm not going anywhere. Not without you. Open. Your. Eyes."

Her head hurt. It was still so dark where she was. Edie could only think to describe this experience as being in limbo. Just lying in that bed, stuck in an unconscious state, as she could hear the voices speaking to her, and feel Tate's hands holding hers. But she could not open her eyes, or respond in any way. She had tried to force her eyes open, time and again, but getting no results became exhausting. So she had slept some more.

This time, the light in the room was bright. When she lifted her eyelids, the brightness felt as if it would blind her. She closed her eyes again and she could feel them watering. She tried again to open her eyes. This time she managed to lift her eyelids open a little farther. She saw Tate. His face looked blurred. She closed her eyes again.

"That's it, that's it, E. Come on…" His voice was so soothing and encouraging, but there was fear in it, too. Edie knew she had worried him.

She was able to hold her eyes completely open now, and her blurred vision began to improve. Tate no longer looked like he had two heads with oblong foreheads. He was as perfect as she remembered now.

"How… long…" Edie began to speak, but her mouth was too dry. She tried to clear her throat and then swallow but that was so uncomfortable.

"Shh…don't try to talk. I'll call for the nurse!" Tate pushed a call button near the bed, and told the responding nurse that Edie was awake.

"Wa…t…er"

"Oh okay," Tate reached for the pitcher near her bed that he had been drinking out of. He poured the iced water into a cup with a straw. He poured it so fast that a few ice cubes bounced out of the cup and onto the floor. He moved to place the straw between her lips, and Edie felt so helpless. She took a slow slip and finally was able to swallow without her throat hurting.

A heavyset middle-aged nurse entered the room just as Tate continued to help Edie take a drink. "Looks like our sleeping beauty is ready to get back to the land of the living…"

Edie tried to smile. She hardly felt like a beauty right now. No makeup. Her hair must be a mess. And her head was throbbing.

"The doctor was paged and will be here shortly," the nurse told Tate and then looked over at Edie. "Is there anything we can get you? I see this good man here got you some water."

"My head hurts," Edie said, reaching up to touch her forehead and immediately felt alarmed when her hand pressed against a thick squared bandage. "What is that?"

"It's okay, Edie. You hit your head in the accident. It's bandaged, but the doctor said it will heal. No worries," Tate tried to reassure her..

"Oh my God, do I have stitches? Am I going to scar?" The old Edie was back and Tate could not help but smile at her.

"It's fine. Just a bump. Let it heal and you will be as good as new. E, with or without a bump and bandage, you are beautiful, but more importantly you are here – you are alive."

"What happened to me?" Edie asked Tate as the nurse checked her vitals.

"You ran off the road in the fog, you hit the ditch pretty hard, and that's when your head met the steering wheel. Do you remember that?" Tate felt so grateful at this moment to have her back. All he wanted to do was look at her, touch her, and talk to her.

"Yes, I think so. I remember a truck in my lane, coming right toward me. There was nothing else I could do, I had to swerve out of the way and get off the road."

"Really?" Tate asked. "You must be a little confused. There was a truck, but the driver of it was behind you. He said he saw you run off the road so he stopped and called for emergency."

"That's not how it happened. Not at all...no!" Edie became agitated and the nurse looked at Tate and slowly shook her head.

"I'm sure it's all a little fuzzy in your mind right now. Just try not to think too much about it. It'll come back clearly after a little time," the nurse told her. "And, sometimes, honey, it doesn't matter if those details remain unclear. You went through a traumatic event. The important thing is you are okay, you know who you are, and you recognize your man here."

"She's right," Tate told Edie, reaching for her hand again. "This is all that matters. You came back. And you're going to be okay."

Okay wasn't exactly how Edie felt when the doctor was examining her and she noticed Tate had been on his cell phone. Edie was told by the doctor that she had to remain in the hospital for a twenty-four observation before being released to go home. Once they were alone in the room again, Edie spoke first.

"Who were you texting a few minutes ago?" she asked him, and he liked the fact that she was interested in what he was doing. The two of them had gotten so comfortable sharing life together that those little things had often gone overlooked. He had done his thing and Edie was wrapped up in hers. Tate was hoping something good would now come out of this accident. Their eyes were opened to how fleeting life can be. Every moment defies time. And it was time for them to hold onto to their lives a little tighter. Be a little wiser to their blessings. And appreciate each other more. That is the way Tate felt about his life now. Losing his father and now experiencing this scare with Edie had greatly affected him.

"I let Syd know you are going to be okay..." Tate smiled. And Edie felt her own heartbeat quicken, and she knew her face flushed.

"Is she coming here?" Edie asked, feeling and sounding defensive.

"Maybe, if she can step away from the market," Tate replied. "Look, Edie, I know the two of you aren't super close, but maybe you both should work on that a bit now. Second chances can change things. Syd has been here so much, as worried about you as I was."

"I'll bet," Edie replied. She had a fire inside of her now. She laid back on the stiff pillow that had a molded spot right in the center where her head had been pressed against for days. She thought about her experience while she was unconscious. *She had seen and was with Tate's father. He led her on a journey. The present. The past. Was any of that real? Did her sister really try to have her killed?* Edie wondered who would believe it. She wasn't even sure at this point if she believed it herself.

Chapter 7

By that evening, Edie was having a difficult time keeping her eyes open. She and Tate had been sharing conversation, meaningful words that neither of them had offered in a very long time. They wanted a future together, both of them were certain of that. Tate had told her he loved her, and Edie smiled, touched his hand and then held it for the longest time. She never could say it back. If she had said those words before to him, she didn't remember when.

"You need to get some rest," Tate told her, as he watched her heavy eyes close and then open again.

"Only if you promise to go home tonight and get some real sleep in a bed." Edie knew he had not left her side in days.

"Not without you," Tate told her. "We'll do that tomorrow night after you are released from this joint."

"Nonsense. I will rest better knowing you are not trying to curl up on that hardback chair for another night," Edie told him. "Please, just go, but come back for me first thing in the morning and take me home."

Tate stood up from the chair beside her bed. He stretched his body, arms in the air, and twisted his torso a few times. Those tight jeans and fitted flannel shirt formed his body. Edie was looking at him, almost as if it was the first time. He was a beautiful man. His sandy brown hair needed a trim, but those loose curls on his forehead, around his ears, and down his neckline were so him. A little unkempt and quite sexy.

"What are you staring at?" he asked her with a grin on his face.

"The sexiest man in the world, and I'm smiling because he's mine…" Tate leaned in and kissed her full on the mouth. It's the first real kiss they shared today since she woke up. And Edie quickly pulled away.

"You cannot want to kiss me now. I am a freaking mess." Edie had a meltdown when she looked in the bathroom mirror just hours earlier. Tate had not been in the room with her at the time. Only a nurse. The nurse didn't understand. She possibly assumed Edie was just vain. It was more than that. Edie had not felt that helpless and scared since the day her parents died. That feeling had come rushing back. And she pushed it away as fast as she possibly could.

"I happen to think you look beautiful. E, the wound will heal. Don't you worry." Tate wished her a good night and made her promise to call him if she wanted him to come back before morning.

Edie was lying in that dark hospital room with her eyes closed. It only seemed like seconds had passed since Tate left. It was five minutes after nine o'clock. Visiting hours were over, and that end of the hospital was quiet. Still, Edie heard every little sound. Machines beeping. Staff walking by. Nurses talking outside of the door at the main desk. She was extremely tired, but could not rest her mind.

A sudden light from the hallway forced her to open her eyes. She saw the door to her room standing wide open and Sydney was there, in the doorway.

Edie jumped and sat upright in her bed. "Syd?" she called out.

"I'm sorry if I startled you..." Edie could see she was wearing that ridiculous burgundy smock with Ry's Market stitched in cursive above the left breast pocket. Those baggy jeans and white tennis shoes also made Edie want to roll her eyes. Her sister always unnerved her.

"What are you doing here?" Edie didn't know what else to say. She was still contemplating accusing her of what she had experienced *–or dreamed–* while she was under.

"I just left work. It's been busy since I took over as store manager. Tate texted me the good news, and I told him I'd be here." Sydney had walked all the way into the room by now and there was only a dim light on as she neared the bed Edie was lying on.

"So are you here because you wanted to keep your word to Tate, or to see me?" The direct, forward nature, was not an unusual exchange between these two sisters.

"You, of course," Sydney answered. "Where is he though?"

"Home, asleep in our bed." It was as if Edie knew those words, *our bed*, would cut to the very core of her sister's being.

"Well he deserves to get some rest," Sydney spoke, defending Tate as usual. "He never left your side since the accident."

"Yes…an accident. My how quickly things can happen. You know, I've driven that damn road time and again, day and night. I just don't see how I just so suddenly ran my car off the road."

"The fog was heavy, Edie," Sydney stated.

"Yes, the fog. But, there was no man driving in a truck behind me. That fucker was in my lane, right in front of me. I swerved to save my life."

Sydney never flinched. "Holy Christ…that's some imagination you have there. Guess it doesn't really matter now. It's over. You're okay." Sydney attempted to close this subject.

"Oh I don't know…I think this is far from over," Edie said, not taking her eyes off of her little sister. *Could she be guilty?*

"Leave it to you to want to reem the guy who pulled over to help you," Sydney stated, and Edie truly wished she could remember what he looked like. She could not recall the man whom she saw speaking to the police or the paramedics. She had been too far away and all she had seen were people in the direct path of the truck beams. She did, however, remember exactly what the man looked like standing in the parking lot of Ry's Market. She could still envision his truck, too. *Were both of those trucks one in the same?*

"I know what I saw, Syd. Let's just leave it at that. For now."

"Yes, let's just leave it," Sydney replied, and a second later a nurse peeked her head into the open doorway and reminded Edie's guest that visiting hours were over.

They exchanged a meaningless goodbye, and Edie lied there awake the rest of the night. She rehashed in her memory where she was and what had happened when she first slipped into unconsciousness. It felt so real. And she was more certain now, than before, that her accident was intentional. Proving it, however, was going to come at a very high cost.

Her story, what Edie believed had happened to her, was going to make others perceive her as crazy. They would focus the blame on the fact that she *hit her head*. No one would believe she saw, spoke to, and spent time with the late Rex Ryman. And who would ever buy into a truth that an innocent, shy, and introverted Sydney Klein would hire a hitman to murder her own sister?

Edie was lying on the sofa in the living room she shared with Tate. He had just settled her onto that sofa which he made into a bed with pillows and blankets. She was holding the remote control but had left the television off. All she had been doing was thinking. Her head hurt from that, too, she believed.

"You're staring at a blank screen. Having troubling turning it on?" Tate asked as he stepped back into the living room. Edie was lounging on the sofa with her hair down because it still pained her to pull it up or back on her head. She was wearing a white fleece sweatshirt and a pair of pink plaid pajama pants with fluffy white socks on her feet. She had yet to cover herself with the blankets Tate had placed on the sofa.

"What?" she asked him.

"The TV?" he asked her, wondering if the doctor was right and he would possibly notice mental signs in Edie's thought process or speech after having a serious head trauma.

"Oh, yes, no I haven't turned it on yet. Just haven't gotten that far," she giggled under her breath.

"You okay? Do you have another headache?" Tate was still worried about her, and he planned to do nothing else but take care of her until she was ready to return to work. A part of him hoped that would be a little while. He loathed how hard she worked and the long hours she spent at the office.

"It's bearable," she said. "I just keep thinking about that night and what all happened." This was her chance. She needed to confide in someone. That confidant obviously could not be her sister. Tate sat down at her feet on the end of the sofa. He rubbed her toes through her thick socks.

"Do you want to talk about what you remember? I mean, what was it like to be in that coma? Could you hear me talking to you, feel me holding your hand? Is that even true what doctors tell us?" Tate had so many questions, and Edie understood, but all she could think about was *where* she had been and *who* she was with while she was in that comatose state.

"I did hear you…it was a voice, your voice, in the distance though. I never felt right there with you. I couldn't always feel your touch. I don't know, it's weird to explain. I tried for what felt like days to come to, and I guess it was that long since you said it took me forty-eight hours to open my eyes. It was a struggle. I was just so exhausted. And then, I went somewhere else. I have memories of being somewhere else." There, she had said it. This was her opportunity to segway to the truth about what had happened to her.

"What do you mean?" Edie had Tate's undivided attention.

"I'm going to tell you something and I want you to listen before you try to understand, or judge me." Edie felt nervous. She folded her hands on her lap, overtop of her pajama pants. Tate nodded his head, trying to conceal his sudden confusion.

He assumed she had her eyes closed for two days to rest her brain. What else could there be? She was asleep. He was there and had witnessed it.

"I remember an oncoming vehicle. I saw the headlights right in front of me. There was no one behind me. I only had a split second to react. I ran my car off of the road to prevent a head-on collision with a truck that was much larger than my car. I remember that much. I know I hit the ditch and then banged by head on the steering wheel. I must have been knocked unconscious immediately. I do remember waking up though."

"You do? The paramedics said you weren't conscious at the scene," Tate questioned her.

"This is where it gets strange. I woke up and I got myself out of the car. I was able to see what was happening around me. It took me a moment, but then I realized I was watching myself, too." Edie paused, as she wanted to make sure Tate understood what she was trying to tell him.

"Are you saying you were out of your body?" He did not appear to think she was talking crazy.

"Yes…I am," Edie answered him. "Believe me, I was really freaked out at first. I thought I had died."

"What did you all see?" A part of Tate did believe this could have been a dream Edie had while unconscious. He also wondered again if she was talking out of her head, as the doctor had put it, because of the possible trauma to her brain.

"I watched the paramedics work. *I* was their emergency. The police were speaking to the other driver of the truck, although I can't remember getting a good look at that man. And I also was able to communicate with someone. He actually came to me at the accident scene." Tate lifted his eyebrows with a confused look on his face. "Tate, I saw… your father."

At that moment Tate stood up from the end of the sofa and paced twice in front of Edie. He ran his fingers through his hair, looked directly at her, and shook his head. "You couldn't have. Pops died. You remember that, don't you?"

"Of course I remember, but your Pops was there with me." Edie never raised her voice or appeared to be adamant. She just calmly told Tate what she believed were true. She saw his dead father.

"Edie, honey, that's not possible." Tate didn't know what else to say. He did not believe her, but he didn't want to upset her.

"I would not believe it either if our roles were reversed right now and you were telling me this," Edie admitted. "But, Tate, I swear to you. He was there. He spoke to me and he led me on a journey to figure things out."

"What the hell?" Tate shook his head at her.

"Just listen…please. This is going to hit you as hard as it did me." Edie looked up at him standing directly in front of her. He seemed intrigued, but also in disbelief. She remembered feeling the very same way.

"Your Pops was wearing pressed jeans, a flannel shirt, and brown-tie shoes. He didn't need a coat out there because he didn't feel the cold. I didn't either, I actually took my coat off outside. You know how I'm always cold!" she added. "He looked so real, he sounded so real. He told me I was going to be okay because I panicked. I thought I was dead, too. I saw your father, spoke to your father. It was your Pops, Tate. I swear."

"What did he say to you?" Tate asked her, showing no emotion, giving her no indication that he either believed her or did not.

"He told me that I had to stay with him for a little while because he was sent to help me figure out a few things…" Edie distinctly remembered Mr. Ryman saying those words to her.

"Well did you figure out something, do you know what he meant by that?" Again, Tate was playing along, but he was uncertain if he believed what Edie was telling him. He was suddenly worried that Edie's head injury was more serious than the medical professionals realized.

"Unfortunately, yes," she answered. "He took me to the market. It was closed, but Syd was still there, working in the office. I watched her and it was so strange being that close and she could not see me. That's when you called her to tell her about my accident. Her reaction was not a panic – and we both know Sydney gets frazzled pretty easily about almost everything. I thought maybe she was in shock. She did leave and I, along with your father, followed her into the parking lot. She wasn't alone. A man was waiting for her. He got out of a pickup truck. He told her she owed him the money for running me off the road." Tate's face fell, and Edie kept talking, wanting to get all of it out before he reacted. "Syd was angry. She told him she would only give him half the money, and he would get the rest when I die."

"This is ridiculous!" Tate blurted out. He would not stand there and listen to an accusation against an innocent person like Sydney. She was Edie's sister for chrissakes.

"Tate. I know what I saw and what I heard. I was there!" Edie was adamant. She knew she would have to defend herself and what had happened to her. She was prepared for Tate not to believe her. She understood how crazy this all sounded. But, even still, she had to tell him.

"You need to take a step back here. Way back. You suffered a head injury that may have been more serious than we all thought. I think we need to get you back to the hospital…" Tate carefully suggested.

"No, I'm fine. Please. It's a lot to process. Too much, I know. Just see me through this, Tate, please."

"So you're asking me to side with you against Syd? I don't know if I can do that. It's just not right. I tried to believe that you saw my Pops. I wanted that to be true. I wanted a sign to know he made it safely to the other side. But, your sister plotting murder? *Your* murder? I don't believe you, Edie."

Chapter 8

Tate stood looking out of the picture window in the living room. He stared at the high-back rocking chairs on his front porch, painted the same cobalt blue as the pillars and the window shutters. He looked far out into the front yard that stretched for two acres. He kept his back to Edie, still lying on the sofa. He didn't know what to say to her. Believing her ridiculous story was just too much for her to ask of him. People were going to get hurt and be embarrassed. He didn't want to drag his mother through this nonsense that would only cause her pain when her grief was still so terribly raw. And Sydney, especially, didn't deserve to be falsely accused.

"Say something, please," he heard Edie say behind him. Her voice was barely a whisper, and he knew she was upset.

"That's just it...I don't know what to say," Tate admitted, turning away from the window and looking at her from across the room. "I really think you need to rest. Maybe in a few days you will have a clearer understanding of what really happened – or did not happen."

"Maybe you're right," Edie replied, deciding it had been a mistake to confide in Tate. It was too soon. She needed proof. She would work to get that proof, and then Tate would believe her.

"Of course, I'm right," Tate tried to smile at her. "Now lay back, close your eyes, and sleep for awhile. I'm sure getting some rest is exactly what will help." Edie did as Tate suggested when he covered her up to her chin and kissed her gently on the cheek. She closed her eyes, but she did not drift off to sleep. And when Tate left the room, she opened her eyes, stared at the ceiling and began to plot her next move.

That night, Edie dreamed of the accident. First, it was her, behind the wheel, in the fog, and those truck headlights were coming right toward her. Then, that same dream, shifted to Edie and Sydney in the backseat of their parents' car. In the dream, just as in real life when she was fourteen years old, Edie could hear the tires screeching, metal crashing, glass breaking, and her mother screaming. The car her family was riding in had flipped once, at least. Edie could see, feel, and hear all in that terrifying moment again, and then everything went dark.

Her eyes opened abruptly. Edie sat upright with a start, and her head instantly pained her. Tate woke up, sat up beside her, and wrapped his arm around her. "What is it?" he asked her in their dark bedroom. She had been tossing and turning all night long. Tate knew, because he had been awake beside her. What she said earlier still worried him. Edie was not the type of woman to just drop things. He knew she would want to get to the bottom of it.

"It's nothing," she replied. "Just a dream and I startled myself, sat up too quickly, and now my head hurts."

"Should I get you some water or something?" Tate asked her, wondering if she needed a painkiller. He rubbed her bare back as Edie always slept completely naked on top of white flannel sheets and a matching down duvet. Tate was beside her wearing only navy blue boxer shorts.

"No," she replied, inhaling a deep breath through her nose as her rapid heartbeat began to calm. Her long blonde hair was down, covering her bare shoulders. "Just hold me." Tate could never remember a time when Edie had been needy like this. A part of him liked it. Before the accident, Edie was a woman who could take care of herself. Her independence, however, had sometimes bothered Tate. He wished for her to slow down and enjoy life more. If there was anything positive that would come out of Edie's accident, maybe it would be this.

Edie taking the time to appreciate life. Tate placed their pillows upright against the missionary oak wood headboard behind them, and then he guided her closer to him and reclined back. Edie pulled up the sheet and duvet over her bare chest, and while Tate held her, she drifted off to sleep again.

    Edie was still asleep at sunrise when Tate slipped out of bed. He took a shower in the hall bathroom so he would not risk waking Edie while running the water in the master bathroom. He dressed inside of the walk-in closet in jeans, a navy blue t-shirt and a matching flannel shirt. He carried his thick white socks out into the kitchen and pulled out a chair by the table where he put them on. He skipped coffee or any breakfast, grabbed his truck keys, cell phone, and wallet off of the countertop, and slipped into his Timberlands out in the mudroom before leaving the house.

    As he drove off, he thought he should have left a note for Edie. He remembered seeing her cell phone charging on the kitchen counter, so he sent a text that he knew would not wake her. *Making a quick trip to the market. Please rest. Text me if you want me to bring you anything before I head back home.*

    Tate drove straight to the market and arrived just before seven o'clock. He grabbed a cup of coffee from the café area inside of the store that offered donuts and other ala cart breakfast items daily. He shared a little small talk with the employee working behind the counter. He knew her name was Dottie. She asked him how his girlfriend was doing –because everyone in town had heard about her one-car accident in the fog– and Tate replied that she was doing *well*.

When he walked away he responded to a few *Good Morning Mr. Ryman* greetings as he made his way straight to the office. He knew Sydney was already in the building because he had seen her hybrid in the parking lot.

The door was closed and he opened it and walked in without knocking, as most of the employees did. It was a confined location where a wall of lockers, a shelf with time cards and a time clock were displayed, and then there was that small desk with a laptop on it in the corner. And that's where Tate found Sydney. She never looked up when he opened the door and walked in. He imagined she dealt with interruptions all day long. He had when he sat in that chair and occupied the manager's position when his father was ill.

Tate walked up behind her, and he noticed she had the bank records displayed on the computer screen. It was not time for payroll for another week, Tate knew, and he had actually stopped by to get the market's financial report for the past month. Tate was staring at the screen over her shoulder when Sydney turned her head and looked up. And that's when she nearly jumped out of her chair.

"Tate! Hi, um, I had no idea you were here." Lately, he never stopped by, and Sydney obviously had let her guard down. Tate immediately picked up on how frazzled Sydney was. Her face flushed, as she spun her chair around to face him.

"I didn't mean to startle you," Tate told her, as he reached over her to place his hot cup of coffee on the desk and Sydney attempted to completely block the laptop screen with the back of her chair. "I'm only here for that," Tate pointed at the computer screen behind her.

"For what?" Sydney asked, and Tate chuckled aloud at her nervous state. He had never known anyone who could become so flustered so easily.

"For the books, Syd. I am going to be spending some time hanging out with Edie at the house this week, to keep an eye on her while she recovers, so I wanted to look over this month's ins and outs."

"Ins and outs?" Sydney asked, realizing she didn't ask about her sister.

"The money coming in and going out," Tate answered her. "I would have called you for the passwords and such, because I can pull up all of it online at home, but I wanted to stop by anyway to see how things are going. I don't want you to think I've left you high and dry."

"Of course I would never think that. It's all going well. I hope you're happy with the job I'm doing. I want to live up to the faith you have in me." Sydney smiled up at Tate. She smiled with her eyes and her entire face. And he never picked up on the way she smiled, the way she always looked at him. Tate couldn't see that Sydney had it so bad for him. It was beyond a crush. It was an obsession.

"I'm more than happy, Syd. This is good for both of us." *Us.* Sydney focused on that one little word. Tate took out a key-ring from the front pocket of his jeans, and he found a tiny key in the middle and inserted it into the top desk drawer. There were papers in there that had his father's handwriting all over them. One, alone, had all of his passwords. It was an old school way of doing things, but that was Rex Ryman. Tate pulled out his cell phone and took a photograph of those passwords. The one for the bank was the third number listed, and he thought the others may be useful later.

While Tate closed the drawer and locked it again, Sydney rolled her chair toward the desk and reached for the keys on the laptop to minimize the screen she had displayed. The chances of Tate walking in now were unbelievable, and her heart had finally begun to beat at its regular rhythm again.

"Okay," Tate said, backing up from the desk, but remaining in the small office with Sydney. "So everything is afloat? Any problems or concerns?"

"Absolutely no worries," Sydney told him. "Business is steady as usual, and I'm working on the orders for a half a dozen catering dates this month. It's busy, but it's all good. I don't mind."

"Well I knew you wouldn't mind, but you gotta make time to have some fun, too. Don't consume yourself with work. You hear?" Tate wondered if his words would sink in. Edie had never understood. She, in the last two years, had become the most productive and successful account executive in Dover, but all of those days and nights of working nonstop had taken a lot away from their relationship. Tate and Edie could not get that time back, but all he wanted to do now was convince Edie to work less once she was well again. This was going to be a new beginning for them. He still had the engagement ring for her. It was just tucked away in a dresser drawer, and one day very soon, he wanted to put it on her finger and plan for their future together.

Sydney giggled nervously. She never had much of a social life, and her plan now was to work incredibly hard in her new position as the store manager of Ry's Market. That was going to be her way to get Tate's attention, not just his appreciation. If he would have been five minutes earlier, Tate would have caught her attempting to delete bank records. It was the only way to hide the fifty-thousand dollar withdrawal from Ry's account. And, now, Sydney would have to steal another five-thousand from the market's account. Another thug needed to be paid for showing her how to hack into the online records of Camden Community Bank.

Tate grabbed his coffee cup off of the desk and started to sip it. "So how's she doing?" Sydney asked him, referring to Edie.

"Pretty good," Tate responded, but what he really wanted to say was *I'm worried about her.* But he couldn't, because the reason he was concerned to the point of being upset was because of Edie's accusation against Sydney. A part of Tate wanted to tell Sydney all about this craziness from the moment he walked into that office. "You should come over. You know, for a visit."

"I doubt my sister wants to see me," Sydney replied.

"And why would you say that?" Tate asked, his curiosity peeking.

"We just aren't close, you are well aware of that. And, I guess, I'm just tired of trying with her." Once again, Sydney's negativity surprised Tate. No matter how often Edie had cut her down or made her feel unwelcome in her life, Sydney always came back. Tate momentarily thought about that. That was exactly why Edie was accusing Sydney of trying to kill her. It wasn't because Sydney would ever turn on her, it was because of Edie. It was possible that Edie was carrying guilt from their relationship, year after year. And when she was unconscious, her subconscious had spoken to her. Tate sat there thinking, analyzing, and staring past Sydney as he slowly sipped coffee.

"What are you thinking about so intently?" Sydney felt bold enough to ask him.

"Oh, just how sometimes things in life have to be dealt with. Nothing ever truly goes away, no matter how bad we want it to," Tate attempted to explain.

"I'm not sure I follow you…" Sydney admitted.

"I actually just now am beginning to understand it myself," Tate replied vaguely. "I'll fill you in sometime, kid," Tate said, getting off the desk. "See you soon. Again, stop by the house. We will be there."

When Tate closed the door, Sydney sat back in her chair and sighed. *Kid? I'm not a fucking kid.*

And one day, Sydney believed, Tate would see that. She was not taking one risk after another for nothing. It was all for him. For them. For the *us* that they were going to be.

Chapter 9

When Tate closed the office door behind him, his text alarm sounded on his cell phone. He had his coffee cup in one hand and retrieved his phone from his pocket with the other.

Hey handsome, please bring me something unhealthy from that café if you're still at the market. You know…like a jelly donut.

An emoji smiley face with a wink followed that text from Edie, and Tate smiled. First, he could hardly believe his eyes. Edie not starving herself or only eating a salad and drinking a glass of wine was a good start. He marched off, through the store, to buy her that jelly donut.

When Tate made his way through the mudroom, he untied and slipped out of his boots before moving up the steps into the kitchen, and he instantly saw Edie sitting at the table. "Hey...how are you doing?" He saw that she was wearing her favorite white terrycloth robe, and her hair was pulled up into a knot, high on her head. He also noticed she no longer had her forehead bandaged. He stepped closer, placed the white paper bag with the jelly donut in it, on the tabletop in front of her. Her forehead was still somewhat swollen and badly bruised. Tate was staring when Edie spoke.

"Better," Edie replied. "My hair pulled up no longer pains me, and as you can see what's underneath the bandage is nasty looking, but it will heal."

"That's my girl," Tate spoke, as he sat down on the chair next to hers and reached for her hand. And then she reached for the bag he brought with him.

"Let me justify eating this sinful little thing," she said, pulling the donut out of the bag and taking a generous bite from it. She chewed gracefully while she spoke. "I figure since I have not eaten for what? Three days now? I can afford these calories."

"Of course you can," Tate told her. "Maybe it's time to give up living on leafy greens." He winked at her, but he was hardly kidding. He wanted her to give up a lot of things. *Working too much. The vengefulness between her and Syd.*

"I'll give it a week," she told him, but once the doctor releases me to return to work, I'll have to get back to the gym was well. You know you only want me for my body." Edie thought she was teasing him, but Tate grew serious.

"Your body is amazing, E. You know that. You also must know that what I feel for you is worlds more than lust and desire. I would never have asked you to share this house, my life, with me if I didn't love you." There it was again. That word, that feeling. It terrified Edie more than she would ever admit.

"Awe Tate. You have my heart," she told him, as she took another bite of the donut, and licked the cherry jelly off of her finger. "Thank you for being here with me. You know I'll go stir crazy until the end of the week." Edie still had four days before her doctor's appointment, which was when she had her heart set on being released to return to normal living. And normal living for Edie was working an eighty-hour week.

After a few minutes of silence, while Edie ate the rest of her donut, Tate spoke again. "I saw Syd when I was at the market this morning. She asked how you're doing…"

"What did you tell her?" Edie asked him.

"I invited her to come visit you, to see for herself," Tate admitted.

"I'll bet you did." Edie knew her sister would not have come around near as much, on weekends, on holidays, if it hadn't been for Tate always extending an invitation to her. Edie had called on her sister a time or two, as well. But, not anymore.

"So are you feeling any different about what you thought you saw…and heard…when you were unconscious?" Tate believed Edie's mindset had changed. The story was entirely too ridiculous to support. She really had no other choice but to drop it. That's the way Tate perceived it.

"Do you really want to bring this up? Come on, Tate, we have days to spend in this house together. I don't want to waste it arguing with you." Edie looked over at him, and at that moment, in her eyes, Tate knew. She had not given up. She was not backing down. She still believed his father had come back from the dead to lead her to some absurd truth about Sydney being a dangerous person. She still felt certain her sister had tried to kill her. Tate took a long, deep breath, and sat back on his chair. He put his arms behind his head, and his elbows were pointing outward.

"I don't want to argue with you either," Tate agreed. "I just want you to come to your senses. You are a smart women, Edie. Realize what you are asking me to believe. It's impossible. It's absurd. It's going to destroy the very little bit that's left of your relationship with your sister."

"I'm sitting here listening to you and it's so hurtful to know that you do not believe me." Edie forced back the feeling of wanting to cry. She was tougher than that. "Yes, I am smart, I am smart enough to know the difference between something that is real and something that is fabricated. I know what happened to me. I saw your father. I witnessed what my own sister did to me. I'm not letting this go." Edie stood up from the kitchen table, and she immediately realized that she moved too quickly. Her head and the stabbing pain above her eyes alerted her.

She stood still for a moment. Tate was watching her, but he never realized she could have been in pain. He was too angry over this. "So that's it? You're going to chase down this crazy notion only to cause other people pain and yourself embarrassment?" Tate ran his fingers through his unruly curls and looked up at Edie again.

"I am going to do what I have to do," she replied.

"Like you always have, huh?" he asked her with sarcasm in his voice. "It's easy, I suppose, when you don't love…" Tate caught himself wanting to say more, to express the rest of what he sometimes believed.

"Don't love what? My sister? I never said that," Edie defended herself, because right now it didn't feel as if anyone else would.

"That's right," Tate said to her with a look in his eyes that Edie never recalled seeing before. It was anger, stemming from pain. "You never, not once, have said it, have you Edith Carmichael Klein? I have told you in the heat of passion, on a lazy Sunday morning drinking coffee and reading the newspaper, when you're dressed to the nines, and when you're fresh out of the shower in your favorite terrycloth robe like right now. I've seen the embellished version of you with makeup galore and expensive clothing and fashionable shoes. I've also seen the bare bones you. I absolutely love both versions. I love all of you. I am in love with you. Does that not mean a fucking thing to you when I say those words?" Edie was fighting harder not to cry. Her head hurt so badly from the pressure. But, she just couldn't do it. She would not cry. And she would not allow herself to say *I love you* back to a man who had given her so much.

When Tate stood up from the table, his chair flew back so fast it tipped over and landed on the tile floor with a loud bang. He just left it when he walked out of the room. He also left Edie standing there alone. She closed her eyes and willed away the unshed tears. It's not that she was incapable of loving him. She just would not allow herself to.

Chapter 10

Hours went by as they shared space in the same house. Tate knew he would come around. He always did. What was said or done was forgotten, and the two of them went on with their lives together. He was sitting on the top step in the mudroom. He was about to put his boots on and take a walk out to the detached garage. But, now, he just left his boots off and sat there in silence. The last he saw Edie she was laying on the sofa in the living room with her eyes closed when he had walked through the room. Whether she had really been asleep or not, Tate didn't know or dwell on it.

He looked out of the window that spanned the entire wall of the mudroom. He noticed a car turn onto his lane road, and when it came closer, he saw it was Sydney's hybrid. Tate stayed where he was as he knew she would use the mudroom entrance to the house. Everyone did. Except for unwanted solicitors. They always walked up those half a dozen wide concrete steps that had no railing on the sides, and up onto the porch to reach the doorbell of the front entrance.

Tate watched Sydney get out of her car. She was always wearing her burgundy Ry's Market smock, this time with a warm white turtleneck underneath it. She wore that smock like a badge of honor. Tate smiled to himself. *She was a character. So unlike Edie.*

"Oh! Hi," Sydney said, as she opened the door from the outside and immediately noticed Tate sitting there. Tate noticed she had gotten a haircut. Her auburn hair, just above her shoulders was wavy and she now had bangs, which he thought made her look somewhat childish. "Are you on your way out? You said I should stop by anytime. I hope it's okay." Sydney always could rattle off three or more sentence together that always made Tate stop to think about which question or statement he should address first.

"Come in. You're fine," Tate smiled.

"Is my beautiful sister inside?" Sydney smirked.

"You're being sarcastic, why?" Tate called her out.

"I'm not really, I just know that a nasty bump on her vain head will make her hide out for awhile. God forbid someone would see an imperfection on her…" Sydney's honesty was harsh, but Tate understood where she was coming from. Always walking in her sister's shadow. And never feeling the love from her.

"Be nice," Tate chuckled, "And, yes, she's inside. Asleep, I think."

"I'll go in to see her in a minute. First, I need to talk to you," Sydney stated. "The bank called. Apparently their online system has been hacked."

"What the hell? Really? I'm surprised I didn't get notified," Tate frowned.

"I'm the point of contact for the market now," she reminded him, and he nodded. "And I told them I would fill you in." Sydney stood in the middle of the mudroom, with her hands in the pouch-like pocket on the front of her smock. "The market's money was untouched, but the account's numbers are screwed up. Apparently the hacker's attempt shifted withdrawals and deposits without being successful at actually stealing anything. The bank just wanted me to relay to you that it's going to take awhile for the numbers to show up correctly." It was lame, but Sydney was so convincing that Tate never second guessed her. He trusted her.

"Oh Christ, how confusing. I have not taken a look at the books yet, but I was going to. Thanks for saving me from freaking out." Tate shook his head and Sydney giggled with a concealed sigh of relief. She had just bought herself some time.

"Not a problem," she replied, but it was a problem. Sydney only had so much time to get thousands of dollars back where it belonged in the Ry's Market account. She had absolutely no idea how she was going to do that, but she did know how to buy time. Tate believed her story. And part of it was true. The bank already became wise to the fact that some of their online accounts had been hacked, and had released a statement to alert its customers. Apparently, Sydney was not the only one playing dirty, as other accounts were compromised too. She was just naïve enough to believe she would not get caught. Hackers went untraced all of the time.

"You can go on in if you want," Tate tilted his head in the direction of the doorway behind him. He had left the kitchen door open while he sat there.

"How is she doing?" Sydney asked him. "Is she feeling up for visitors?"

"You're not a visitor. You're her sister. And I wish you two would act like it sometimes." Tate was still hurting from their argument this morning.

"Yeah, me too," Sydney agreed, because what else could she say? "Is there something bothering you? You seem miffed? Did she do something?"

Tate smirked a bit before he replied. "She miffs me a lot, but I get past it. Because I love her." Sydney felt her insides crawl. "Plain and simple, right? For me, it is. But why in the Sam hell is it so hard for her? Have you ever heard her say those words?"

"I love you?" Sydney was quick to form those three little words into a question because what was rolling off her tongue was a truth she carried in her heart for him. She instantly felt her cheeks flush. "Edie doesn't say it. At least not to me,"

Sydney clarified, but she had assumed Edie had poured her heart out to Tate. She would be a fool not to.

"I wish you two were closer for many reasons, but most of all I need to talk to someone who can get inside of her head. She's smart, she's beautiful, but she's so distant most of the time. I want to break through that." Tate was easily confiding in Sydney, but that feeling of having his trust and wanting to be his confidant was bittersweet because she didn't want to hear how badly he wanted her sister.

"I wish I could say that I will talk to her for you," Sydney stated, "but we both know I'm pretty useless in Edie's eyes. I'm the sister who isn't as bright and beautiful. I have no clout with Edie."

"Back up, little lady," Tate told her. "You need to take a good, long look in the mirror. Appreciate those waves in your hair and those bright eyes."

Sydney felt entirely too happy, hearing Tate compliment her. So much so that she wasn't embarrassed and hadn't blushed. "You must not be seeing the body fat," Sydney replied, immediately regretting that she had cut herself down when Tate had just lifted her up.

"Some guys prefer a handful of a woman," Tate responded, and he winked at her. *That look. That wink.* The attention Tate Ryman was giving her was making Sydney swoon. Everything she had done to get to this point was working. *And so worth it.*

Tate may not have seen what he was doing, and how what he was saying affected Sydney, but Edie had. She was standing in the kitchen, against the counter top, listening and watching. She could only see the back of Tate, but she had a clear view of her sister. Sydney never noticed her. The lights were off in the kitchen and the cloudy day in Camden had kept the room dark.

Edie had always recognized her little sister's crush on Tate. She just never paid any mind to it. Not until now. Now she recognized how dangerous her sister's feelings were. *Would a crush…unreciprocated love…or an obsession… lead her to want me out of the picture that badly? Enough to kill me?* Edie's thoughts raced. She wanted to confront Sydney right this instant. But she knew she could not. She would further infuriate Tate. And without any proof, Sydney could deny it all and get away with it.

So Edie chose to claim what was hers. She walked through the kitchen and she stood in the doorway directly behind Tate's back. He was still seated on the step below her feet. When Sydney looked up, that forced Tate to turn around. This was the closest he had been to Edie all day, following their heated argument this morning.

"Hi Syd…what brings you by in the middle of an important work day?" Edie just could not resist slamming her sister with every comment she made.

"My sister, of course," Sydney responded, and Edie felt like saying, *Could have fooled me, you're drooling over my man.* And now it was time for Edie to reclaim Tate. She knew that if she had any power over Sydney and her crazy mindset right now, it was Tate.

Edie placed her foot on the step that Tate was seated on and he moved aside for her. She sat down close, beside him. "We could go inside," Edie suggested, "but I need a change of scenery. This is always a good spot out here." Tate thought how the mudroom and that top step was his preferred spot, not hers, but he humored Edie with a wide smile as she slipped her arm inside of his. She was wearing a white v-neck waffle-knit thermal shirt and a pair of flared gray sweatpants. Her feet were bare, and now cold out there, and her well-manicured toes were painted dark purple. Her long blonde hair was still in a messy knot on top of her head. She wore no makeup and the bruise on her forehead was a mixture of blue, purple, and red, coloring.

"Syd was just telling me how some of the community bank's online accounts were hacked," Tate turned to Edie as he spoke.

"Are you serious?" Edie asked. She must have walked into the kitchen after the two of them were well into their conversation because she definitely missed that topic.

"Yep, I got the call earlier today. Just a warning that some of our accounts could be screwed up for a few days, you know mismatched numbers and such," Sydney explained. "No need to panic if the withdrawals and deposits do not quite add up." Tate sighed a little and shook his head and stated something about how when you're dealing with millions that would be a reason to panic. Edie was well aware of how much money Ry's Market was bringing in. She didn't care concern herself with it though. She made her own fair share of money. What she was focused on now was how Sydney kept biting her upper lip as she spoke. That, as Edie remembered from far back into their childhood, was a sure sign Sydney was lying. As Edie sat there, she tried to chase away the memory that surfaced. She could hear her mother's voice, *"Sydney Elizabeth! You tell me the truth. I know you're fibbing when you bite your lip like that."*

Edie took a deep breath as she continued to stare at her sister. Her mind was racing, and soon she was in the midst of a flashback on the parking lot. *Was it real or not?* That man was demanding a large sum of money from Sydney. She said she only had half of it. Where else would Sydney be able to come up with what Edie assumed was thousands of dollars? *Sydney was stealing from Ry's Market. That was how she would prove her sister's guilt.*

Sydney now caught herself biting her upper lip. She also saw how Edie was staring at her. They were not at all close, but they did know each other well. Mannerisms and all. "I should go!" Sydney spoke abruptly and somewhat nervously.

"Already? You don't wanna come inside for awhile?" Tate asked her as he stood up on the step now, and Sydney backed up toward the door to leave.

"Not today, maybe tomorrow. Good to see that you are healing, Edie."

"Thanks…" Edie all but mumbled under her breath as Sydney left abruptly.

Tate giggled as she watched her leave through the window. She made a U-turn on the driveway in her compact hybrid and sped away so fast down the lane road that the rocks flew from underneath her small tires. "She's a piece of work. Always so high-strung."

"That she is," Edie said, standing up to almost meet his height on the step. She felt invigorated. Once Tate was asleep later, Edie planned to find a way to log into the bank's website, and hopefully the Ry's Market's account. Getting the password was her next step.

"Are you hungry?" Tate asked her as he stepped up into the kitchen and then pulled her by the hand to help her up as well.

"Maybe…" Edie said, looking at him, and he recognized that fire in her eyes, as he took a step back and put his hands up.

"Baby, not yet… you have some healing to do." Even though he said those words, he could feel himself harden. This woman, no matter how angry he could be with her, he wanted her. Always.

"I know a way to speed up the healing process…" Edie took a step toward him and slipped her hands underneath the front of his flannel shirt where ends of it overlapped the button fly of his jeans. She opened one button at a time and then she reached for him. It didn't take much for his manhood to spring into her hands.

"Come on, E…" he tried to object.

She giggled and let her hands do the work. Tate pulled her close to him in the dark kitchen and he kissed her full and hard on the mouth. His tongue found hers. She heard him ask, *are you sure*, and then one thing inevitably led to another. His jeans and boxers were at his ankles. His chest was bare. Edie was only in her white bra and matching thong. He pulled her bra over her head without undoing the clasp. He pinched both of her nipples and felt them harden to his touch. He helped her slip off her panties, and he kicked off his jeans from his ankles. They kissed with a mounting passion, they touched with a desire as deep and as curious like if it was their first time. Neither one of them could take another moment of this foreplay. Edie reached for the back of a kitchen chair. She bent her body forward, over it, and Tate came from behind her. She gripped the wood on the back of the chair tightly as she could feel his hands between her legs. He then spread her legs further apart and entered her. His thrusts were more gentle than usual, because he was concerned about thrashing her around too roughly so soon following the accident. The way he was taking his time on her –so slowly– further aroused her. In and out with the full length of him. Repeatedly. Edie could feel how wet she was between her legs when she cried out his name after she came explosively with him inside of her. Two more, much harder thrusts later, and Tate was a man satisfied. Again.

Chapter 11

Their clothes were still scattered on the kitchen floor, and the two of them were back in the bedroom, lying naked on their bed. The sheets and duvet were not pulled back. It was just their bodies, entangled, keeping each other warm.

Tate again had his hands on her, and she laughed at him. "I thought we already did that in the kitchen," she reminded him.

"Come again for me," he said to her as he touched her with two of his fingers between her legs. "I want to help you do that again…"

Edie's mind was not on sex, not more of it right now anyway. She had forced herself to completely focus on what they were doing in the kitchen earlier. She enjoyed sex, and Tate was beyond desirable, but her mind was on Sydney and had been ever since she left their house. Edie wanted to talk about Ry's bank account. She wanted Tate to be relaxed, and she knew sex always did that for him. But, now, he wanted to please her again. Edie obliged. She would do anything at this moment to find the proof that she did not have just a dream while she was unconscious. She was not out of her mind to pursue this. Things were beginning to add up, and Edie believed her sister was the crazy one to think she would get by with this.

Edie's head was hurting and she wanted to rush this. She placed her hand on top of Tate's between her legs, and moved it aside, and he knew what she was doing. He stopped, and he watched her take over. She started to pleasure herself, and as Tate often did at this moment, he grabbed his cell phone off of the nightstand on his side of the bed. And he recorded a video of Edie. It was a high and pure arousal for him to replay it later – and then he would delete it. At the moment, Edie felt like Meg Ryan in the restaurant scene from the movie, *When Harry Met Sally*. She totally put her all into the moaning, the motions, and in the end she had faked an orgasm for Tate.

They were in the kitchen, eating pizza that they had delivered to the house. Edie forced herself to stop after having one piece and taking two bites of another. She needed to maintain her figure and this recovery was not helping as she had not been working out or counting calories.

When she pushed her plate forward, Tate glanced at her. "Full already?"

"I've had more than enough, thanks babe." Edie replied. And then she brought up what was on her mind. *The hacking crisis at the bank.* "So, do you think Syd is right? Does the bank have everyone's money where it should be by now?"

"Oh I hope that will be the case eventually," Tate replied. "I'm just relieved that Ry's money wasn't stolen." The idea of little old Mrs. Ryman having millions of dollars in her own personal bank account and more millions in the market's account was fascinating to Edie. If she were Mary Lou Ryman, she would start to enjoy that money at seventy-five years old. It was now or never. *Take trips. Buy an expensive wardrobe. Live in a mansion for God's sake. Have houses in other states, or countries.* Mrs. Ryman was just not the type of woman to enjoy anything too extreme. She never flaunted. One day, Tate and his sister would see that money in their names. Edie knew Tate's sister, Kathy was greedy for it. Tate, on the other hand, preferred to live simply. He had a nice house on a decent piece of land, an expensive truck, and nothing else, material-wise, mattered to him. He was happy wearing denim, boots, and flannel shirts.

"Exactly, me too," Edie replied, not feeling all that certain it wasn't.

After Tate fell asleep, and she was sure he was sound, Edie took his cell phone off of the nightstand on his side of the bed. Earlier, she had reminded him to *delete the porn off of his phone* and he commented slyly about the possibility of keeping that one. Edie was going to take care of that decision for him. She swiped his screen, retrieved the video and then trashed it. She unintentionally swiped the screen again and noticed the most recent photograph Tate had taken. It was like hitting the jackpot, winning the highest lottery. Exactly what she needed was right there in her hands. Edie sent the photograph containing the password to the market's bank account to her own cell phone. And then she deleted the evidence of that from Tate's phone. She left his phone on his nightstand and walked quickly around their bed to grab hers off the nightstand on her side of the bed. She immediately went into the living room, sat down on the sofa, and powered on the laptop that was placed on the coffee table. She had attempted to work from it earlier in the day, but had to stop when a headache persisted.

She felt nervous. Tate would be so angry with her if he caught her, if he knew what she was doing. Her hands were clammy, and her heartbeat had quickened. The password, *T-REX*, was immediately accepted and Edie found herself staring at a lot of numbers. She hated math, she struggled with the ins and outs of understanding a statement like this. She only knew she was looking for a large sum of money going out. It would have to be a lot, considering the market had bills to pay that were hardly minimal. She couldn't believe that Tate had put Sydney, of all people, in charge of something so dire in a successful company. And she had betrayed him, and his family. The family that she claimed to care about.

Nothing caught Edie's eye as she scrolled through every withdrawal in the past month. And, then, when she reached the third page, she froze. Fifty thousand dollars. And, in the memo column, there was a blank. *Who was the recipient of this large sum of money?* If Tate had seen this transaction, he would have instantly been alarmed, Edie thought to herself, and Sydney knew that. That was why she made up that lame excuse about the bank's accounts being hacked. *Or maybe the bank was aware, and still looking for the culprit?* Well, Edie knew who the culprit was in this. Her hands were shaking now. And, she could have cried if she would have allowed the tears to surface. If she doubted herself at all, if she wondered even the slightest bit about her *experience* following her accident being factual, she was completely certain now. *Sydney had hired someone to kill her.* And, now, Edie was going after her. The idea that she was her sister, her only family left in this world, mattered none. *And why should it? Sydney had gone too far. She was out of her mind.*

Chapter 12

Just as it happened all day long, Sydney heard someone come into the cramped office space when she was punching the keys in front of the computer at Ry's Market. She assumed the person behind her would get what they needed and leave again. That's exactly why Sydney preferred to work late at night, alone, after the store's closing hours. She was a classic introvert and anti-social for sure.

After at least a few minutes, or more, had passed, Sydney was overcome with the feeling that someone was staring at her. She spun her chair around, and then looked behind her. Her eyes widened immediately. This was the last person she would ever expect.

"Oh, my, Mrs. Ryman, hello," Sydney all but stuttered. "I had no idea it was you who came in. I would not have kept you waiting. You should have made your presence known." Sydney had always been kind to this woman. She was, after all, her boss. The only superior in the workforce, along with Mr. Ryman, that Sydney had ever known. Sydney liked her. And, Mary Lou, in turn, had been nothing but cordial.

Mary Lou stood there in a pair of gray slacks and a pale pink sweater. Her black wool peacoat was draped over her arm, and she was wearing black Mary Janes with thick natural colored nylons on her tiny feet. She was a petite woman who had aged considerably, Sydney thought, in the past decade she had known her. Maybe most of that aging had taken place in recent years when she cared for her ailing husband. A husband who was six years her junior.

"Hello, Sydney, dear," Mrs. Ryman replied. "I hope you have a minute for me? I know my son tells me how hard you are working for us…"

Sydney smiled. *Tate had been talking about her to his mother?* That was such a high for her right now, to hear that, to know that. Sydney's smile was wide and Mrs. Ryman never took her eyes off of her.

"Do you want to sit down?" Sydney offered, but before she stood up to retrieve that one metal chair folded up against the far wall, Mrs. Ryman stopped her.

"No, thank you, I am fine. I will stand while I tell you what I came here to say." Mrs. Ryman was calm and stoic, as most people only saw her. Even at the funeral for her husband, she remained entirely composed. Sydney nodded her head.

"I have good friends who work for me in this store," she began. "And it is *my* store now. My husband wanted Ry's Market to be in my name only after he was gone since both of my children are not interested in owning the family business. That saddens me, sure, but *it is what it is* as my grandchildren have taught me to say." Mrs. Ryman smiled, but it faded as quickly as it surfaced. "Anyway, as I mentioned, I have good friends who work for me." Sydney remained quiet, just sitting in her chair, with her hands on her lap. She wondered if Mrs. Ryman was there to thank her, or if she was implying that she was one of those good friends. If so, Sydney would be nothing but honored to know Mrs. Ryman felt that way. "Tommy Kampwerth, who stocks shelves on Mondays and Thursdays, is very dear to my heart. He's my age, seventy-five, and we went to school together. He actually took me to homecoming, years before I started courting Rex." Sydney smiled. Mrs. Ryman was rambling, and Sydney really didn't have all the time in the world to listen, but she remained respectful. She almost wished Tate would walk in at this moment and see the two of them together. She was sure to gain points with him then. She was also certain Edie never exchanged more than a few meaningless words with Tate's mother.

"I know Tommy well, Mrs. Ryman," Sydney spoke honestly. She was fond of the gentleman who worked only in aisles three or seven, where it took him all day to stock shelves, partly because he chatted with every shopper who passed by.

"Well good," Mrs. Ryman said to her. "I doubt you are aware that he is a computer whiz. He loves the World Wide Web, as I believe it's called." Sydney let out a slight giggle at that comment. "Tommy keeps an eye on this store for me. He came to my house with his portable computer last night. It seems the numbers that he checks each month in my market account are not adding up. We called the bank together and there seems to be an outsider horning in on my business. Stealing my money…"

Sydney immediately began to drum up the story in her mind. It would be the same one she fed Tate. Hacking was discovered, but Ry's Market account was safe, despite what the numbers showed. *Jesus. That sounded so lame to her right now as she rehashed it in her head. Especially since Mrs. Ryman had said she called the bank.*

But before Sydney could utter a rehearsed word, Mrs. Ryman spoke again. "I have not gone to my son, nor have I contacted the authorities. I am standing here for answers, and you had damn well better give them to me." Sydney was certain this woman rarely, if ever, cursed. It actually sort of frightened her. *Maybe this frail little old woman was deceiving on the exterior and should be feared?* Sydney tried her absolute best to remain calm.

"I understand your concern," Sydney began. "I can assure you I have spoken to the bank president and the market's money is safe. Yes, there were accounts compromised at the bank, but your money is safe. The numbers may not show it, and I told Tate the same, but there really is no reason to worry."

She held her breath and awaited Mrs. Ryman's response.

"You must take me for some old fool…" Mrs. Ryman's lips were pursed when she paused, "but I can assure you I am not. I may live a simple life with less extravagant things. I don't need a big house, fancy clothes, or frequent trips. I do like to count my money though. It's a favorite pastime of mine. Oh, and Tommy, as we both speak so highly of, has a grandson. He's a remarkable man, yes. He's Camden's only bank's president."

Sydney felt her face fall. *Was she caught? Was she going to prison for life? Had the money been traced to the thug she paid off in the back alley of Lantern Inn?* And, her ultimate fear, *What would Tate think of her now?*

"You are mistaken, Mrs.-"

"I thought I made myself clear? Do not play me for a fool." Mrs. Ryman's voice remained so calm is was almost eerie. "Tell me why you stole fifty thousand dollars from me. I will not leave here until the truth comes out of your mouth."

Sydney sighed. *The truth? Where would she begin with this? Should she just blurt out that she wanted her sister out of her life, gone from this world?* "I will pay you back every last cent. That was my plan. I just needed time."

"Are you in trouble?" Mrs. Ryman asked Sydney, and she assumed she meant financially. This old lady had absolutely no idea what kind of trouble Sydney had recently gotten herself into.

"I feel like I am now," Sydney admitted, and she surprised herself with those honest words.

"Let me share something with you," Mrs. Ryman said. "I have millions of dollars, as you now know because my son trusted you with our business. I do not need a measly fifty thousand dollars. In fact, I wonder now if I would have even loaned it to you if you had asked, if your reasoning behind needing that much money was necessary to your survival or something."

"Necessary to my survival?" Sydney repeated, feeling strong and so unlike herself right now. But, it was now or never. She would plead her case, or at least share the truth that had been eating away at her for so very long. "My, how that's an interesting way to phrase it. My parents, as you probably know after living in this town all of your life, were killed in a car accident when I was only eleven years old. From that day on, I tried every way I knew how to get my big sister to love me and take care of me, and to just be my family. She was all I had left. And she failed me. She left me feeling helpless and hopeless and unloved for most of my life. When she was not ignoring me, she was berating me. And that has not changed. I hate her, and I've finally reached the point of no return. I do not want or need her love. In fact, she is in my way of having a great love, a wonderful life. So, you want to know what I did with the money I prefer to say I borrowed from your bank account? I hired a hitman to kill my sister."

Mrs. Ryman swallowed hard. This was shocking, sure. She thought of the accident. She thought how she had not gone to visit that girl in the hospital, nor since she was at home recovering. She did talk to Tate about her, and kindly through clenched teeth she had asked how Edie was feeling, but that was all. She only cared about her son and his state of worry and sadness when he almost lost that woman he's so deeply in love with. Mrs. Ryman would never understand it. But, she had tried to support that relationship for the sake of her son.

"Say something, please..." Sydney begged. "I know you must think I'm a horrible person. I just could not take it anymore...and I wish she had died."

"I never thought I would be standing inside of this office my honest husband used to call his own, under this roof of a store I sometimes thought he loved more than me...never in my wildest dreams had I ever fathomed something like this. In response to what you have told me, I have only one thing to say..." Sydney held her breath.

"If you need more money for someone to finish the job, I will personally write you a check." And then the elderly woman started to turn to walk away. Just like that, she began to exit the office. Sydney thought about calling her back. She wanted to be sure she understood this exchange. What exactly had just gone down? *Mrs. Ryman hated Edie just as much? Enough to also want her dead?*

And then Sydney opted to just let her walk out that door.

Chapter 13

Tate was outside shoveling the snow-packed driveway in front of his detached double-car garage and the walkway that led up the entrance of the mudroom. Two inches of snow had fallen overnight. He had his hood up on his coat as the wind was blustery. Edie was inside, almost ready to leave to take a drive into town. She was not supposed to be driving until she had a follow-up appointment with her doctor. But she felt stronger, and her bruise was healing. Edie had applied a powder-based foundation to her face and forehead this morning. A little makeup to conceal some of the discoloration from the bruise made her feel more at ease about going out in public since the accident. The accident that she was going to discuss with her sister today. It was time. Edie now had the proof to confront her.

Edie was wearing a winter white chunky turtleneck sweater with black leggings, and tall tan Ugg boots. She grabbed her purse and her long winter white coat on her way out of the kitchen and into the mudroom, where she slipped it on and fastened it to prepare for the cold. Tate was still shoveling the snow when he spotted her walking on the path he had already cleared.

"Hey, look at you. You look great. Where are you going?" Tate gave her a look that she interpreted as, *you are not supposed to be driving*.

"For a drive into town," she replied cautiously.

"To where? I can take you. You have not been released to drive yet, E." Tate was a by-the-book man who almost always walked the straight and narrow. It was one of the things Edie never minded too much about him, but in a case like this, it sometimes annoyed her. Right now, however, she opted to just tell him the truth.

"Your mom called," she admitted. "I'm not sure what it's about, but she asked to see me."

"Seriously?" Tate asked, looking perplexed. That was not an everyday occurrence. In fact, it never occurred before at all. Tate's mother had not taken to Edie, and Tate clearly realized that, no matter how she pretended to come across. "Well, I'm going with you. No objections. I'll shovel her walk or something while we're there. My curiosity has peaked." Edie smiled at him, and gave in. She had no idea why Mrs. Ryman had summoned her, and if she really did dwell on it, it made her nervous. If anything, just having Tate there would help calm her nerves.

When they stepped inside, Tate and Edie both dried the bottom of their boots on the rug directly in front of Mrs. Ryman's kitchen door. Her house was a modest bricked ranch-style with a full furnished basement. It was the house she and her husband moved into when their children were small. The market had begun to do well then, and they had lived in the same home ever since.

"Tate? I didn't know you were coming along…" Mrs. Ryman spoke, as she sat at the oval cherry wood kitchen table with a steaming cup of coffee. Compared to Edie and Tate who had just come in from the cold, snowy weather, she looked warm and cozy in her powder blue sweatsuit.

"Edie cannot drive yet, Ma," Tate said, and Edie shook her head as if that was not a big deal. "And I figured you would need me shovel your walk."

"Yes, you go do that," Tate's mother told him, "while Edie and I have a cup of coffee."

"Where's my coffee?" Tate asked, but he was teasing, and Edie smiled at him. He loved his mother. There were times when she saw the interaction between Tate and both of his parents, before his father died, and she would feel an overwhelming sadness for what she did not have in her life. Edie was still standing beside Tate on the rug which was now wet from the clumps of snow on the soles of their boots.

"You'll get yours when you're done shoveling," Mrs. Ryman winked at him, but Tate knew she was serious. For some reason, his mother wanted to speak to Edie alone. He just hoped it was all good. "Come in, dear, and don't worry if your boots are a little wet. Floors will dry." Mrs. Ryman had noticed Edie attempting to wipe off the bottoms of her boots on the rug, shuffling her feet back and forth. She just wasn't in a hurry to move over to the kitchen table and have a conversation with her boyfriend's mother. She and Mary Lou Ryman had never gotten along, or attempted to get to know each other.

Edie watched Tate leave before she finally turned around and walked over to the table. She draped her long coat over one chair and then pulled out another chair adjacent to Mary Lou's. When she sat down, Mary Lou stood up. She walked over to the counter in her brown moccasins which she wore with thick white socks. She poured Edie a cup of coffee and refilled her own cup at the counter before she walked back to the table with both.

Edie thanked her, but said nothing more. Her snow white hair, cut into a bob, always looked the same. Mary Lou's eyes looked different now though, as Edie recognized the grief in them. It was a pain that goes hand in hand with loss. An emptiness that eats away at a person day in and day out. Edie had been there and saw the light missing from her own eyes for many years after her parents were killed. This was the first time Edie felt remotely connected to Tate's mother. She wouldn't speak of it though. She couldn't resurrect that pain inside of her. Not for anyone.

While Edie sipped her coffee, Mary Lou noticed something different in her as well. She looked natural without all of the frill and perfectly applied makeup. She was a beautiful woman on the exterior, for sure, Mary Lou had always recognized that. She saw the bruise on her forehead. Even underneath makeup, it could not be entirely concealed. For a moment, Mary Lou felt sorry for her pain. It had to be awful to have a car accident. Mary Lou was aware it had not been Edie's first, although the crash when she was a child was far worse because it had taken lives. Her parents' lives.

"So, how are you feeling?" Mary Lou asked, referring to Edie's recovery from the accident.

"Better every day, thank you," Edie replied. "I still have to be released by my doctor to go back to work though, and I'm hoping that will be next week." *Ah, yes, her work,* Mary Lou thought to herself. What she wanted most for her son was a woman opposite of Edie. One who didn't worship a career. A woman willing to stay at home and raise babies. Just as Mary Lou had. She never worked a day at their market until after her children were school aged. What she wanted for Tate was so much more than Edie Klein was, and would ever be.

"Have you ever thought about quitting that job of yours?" Mary Lou asked her, and Edie nearly choked on the coffee she had just swallowed. "What I mean is, it appears to consume you. My God, you were on your way home from working so late at night…" This was the first time Mrs. Ryman had not held back. She had never tried to get this girl to change before. She knew if her husband were still alive, he would reprimand her now for what she was doing, for what she was saying to the woman their son loved.

"I know you're hurting," Edie spoke, not even realizing why she was being so honest and not at all feeling angry for this woman's judgmental behavior. Mrs. Ryman only stared at Edie. "You see, I've been there. I know grief and I know what it can do to a person. It really can make you act like you never would otherwise."

"I don't understand," Mrs. Ryman said to her, "and I would rather not discuss my grief for my husband with you."

"Sure. Never mind," Edie obliged. "It's no secret that you don't like me." Edie changed her focus from discussing grief, because that was never a good idea for her. "And that's okay. What matters is how your son feels. He loves me."

"Yes, but do you love him?" Mrs. Ryman was direct and it was so unlike her. Still, Edie was not afraid of this conversation. For once, she was being real. They both were. She felt oddly connected to this woman who she never really liked at all.

Did she love Tate? Why was she being forced to go there again? Admitting her feelings was not her strength. In fact, that act alone made her feel weak. She had decided long ago that feeling too deep, expressing too much, would only drown her. "Tate is very important to me," Edie answered, carefully.

"And what about your sister?" Mrs. Ryman added. "She's your only family. And yet you treat her like a stranger."

Edie was taken aback. "Forgive me, Mrs. Ryman, but how is my relationship with Syd any of your business?"

"I suppose I've reached a point where I am trying to figure you out. I don't like what I see." Mrs. Ryman scoffed at her.

"I think your son would be very upset with you if he heard how you are speaking to me right now." Edie played the Tate card. He, after all, was the man between them. The man in her life was this woman's only son. A grown man, nonetheless, who could make his own decisions.

"Let's leave Tate out of this," Mrs. Ryman responded. Edie still had a full cup of coffee in front of her, which she had not touched since this conversation became more heated than the beverage itself. Mrs. Ryman, on the other hand, had already drank half of hers.

"What exactly is this?" Edie asked. "You called me. I came. What do you want from me?"

"I want you to help me die." Those words, so certain and direct, made Edie's eyes widen, and her mouth dropped open but she was momentarily unable to speak.

"Excuse me? Mrs. Ryman, you really need to see a doctor ...please let me and Tate get you some help." Edie started to stand up, but Mrs. Ryman stopped her. She placed her hand on top of Edie's and held it there. This was the first touch Edie ever remembered from this woman. She had always kept her distance, and Edie liked it that way. This, however, felt genuine. Motherly. The way Mrs. Ryman was toying with her emotions made Edie feel terribly uncomfortable. She should have walked out of this kitchen by now. No one deserved to be treated like this. But something was keeping her there.

"No doctor. I need someone who understands what I'm going through. You know grief. You implied as much earlier."

A part of Mrs. Ryman wanted to understand this young woman. But, the other, dominant part of her just wanted to create a rift between Edie and her son. She wanted Edie to think she was grief-stricken to the point of being suicidal. Mrs. Ryman did not intend for her own life to end. She just wanted Edie to believe that. "You also do not like me much. You're the perfect person to help me die."

Edie was instantly scared. *Tate needed to know this. Tate should be inside of his mother's house right now, hearing this craziness.* But, he wasn't. And she felt forced to handle this. Edie inhaled a deep, slow breath through her nostrils, and hoped to God she was making the right decision by confiding in this woman. Her reckless behavior called for dire measures. Edie suddenly believed she could help Tate's mother. By telling her the truth. *Maybe if she knew her husband had made it to the other side, she would be able to pull herself together, and go on living her life.*

Chapter 14

"I do understand. More than you know," Edie told her. "Just, please, listen and hear me out completely before you respond." Mrs. Ryman only nodded her head, as she took another long sip of her coffee, nearly finishing it all. "When I had the accident, I woke up at the scene. There's no other way to explain it. I had an out of body experience. I watched what was happening to me, and I wasn't alone. Someone was sent from the other side to comfort me, I guess, and to guide me, and help me understand exactly what had happened." Mrs. Ryman creased her brow and she wanted to interject and express her confusion, but she relented and just listened. "It was your husband. I saw him, spoke to him. He was there."

Mrs. Ryman felt herself gasp. Her hand, that she lifted to cover her mouth, instantly began to shake. Tears formed in her eyes. And then she lashed out. "How dare you! I will not let you use my husband's memory like this! Why would he come to you? Why not me? I won't listen to this nonsense!" Mrs. Ryman choked on a sob as Edie persisted.

"I swear to you, it's true. He was real. He looked like himself, his old self. Healthy and handsome." Edie was not sure if she should have so boldly described him as handsome, but she believed he was. He and Tate shared some beautiful features. Mrs. Ryman shook her head, and then bowed it, and held it in her hands. She didn't feel well. This was all too much for her to hear. She didn't believe it. *Why would she? Why would her husband come to Edie of all people? Why had he not come to her? If he was going to cross over from the other side, he would come to her. She was his wife of forty-eight years.*

"I realize this is all too much, but your husband led me on a journey of warning. I know how ridiculous this will sound to you, but my car accident was not something that just happened because of the fog or my inability to keep my car on the road. I was purposely run off of the road. My sister tried to have me killed." There, she had said it. With very little warning, Edie had spoken some awfully shocking words. Words that Mrs. Ryman literally could not handle hearing. Because she now knew it was true. Rex had come back to warn Edie about her sister. *What would Rex think of his wife now?* Mary Lou was ashamed and frightened. *What in God's name had grief done to her?*

The room started spinning. She reached for her empty coffee cup and knocked it over on the tabletop. She was suddenly on the verge of passing out. Edie saw her eyes roll back into her head. Edie quickly stood up, called her name, and caught her by the shoulders when she slumped sideways and nearly fell off the chair. When Edie screamed for Tate, he was just then turning the knob on the door to come back inside.

"Call an ambulance!" Edie shouted, as Tate let the door swing open and it hit the stopper on the wall hard and ricochet back toward him.

"What the hell happened?" he yelled, in full panic mode, as he rushed toward his mother who was limp, and slumped forward.

"She passed out!" Edie was in complete panic mode. She would have to admit to him later that she confessed her secret. And it obviously had been too much for her. If something happened to Tate's mother now, it would be on Edie's hands, and he would never forgive her. Tate was right when he told her that his mother was too fragile in her state of grief. She was easily broken, and Edie had pushed her to the breaking point.

When the paramedics rushed through the door, Edie stood back. Her heart was racing. This was not her intention. She honestly had believed that by telling Mrs. Ryman the truth, she would be able help to her cope in her state of grief. Little did Edie know that this was not Mrs. Ryman's plan either. She had invited Edie into her home for coffee. Coffee that she had spiked with Edie's own prescription pain medicine. Tate and Edie had left the house yesterday at lunchtime. That's when she entered through the unlocked mudroom door and went into the kitchen, where she stole the bottle of pills off of their countertop. The plan was simple, or so it seemed. They didn't need a hitman to take care of Edie. With her own pills in her system, it would be understood. *She was a troubled woman who had not dealt with her painful past,* they would say, *and so she took her own life.*

Only, sometimes, things do not quite pan out as premeditated. Edie never drank more than a sip of the coffee that Mrs. Ryman had set in front of her. It was Mrs. Ryman who had finished every last drop of her own that had mistakenly contained all of the pre-crushed pills. That mix-up was what led Mary Lou Ryman to being the one the paramedics were frantically trying to resuscitate on her own kitchen floor.

Chapter 15

Tate was back in the waiting room at Bayhealth Medical Center, only this time he wasn't alone. Edie was beside him. He was quiet when they first sat down. He already said all that came to mind as they drove well over the speed limit behind the ambulance transporting his mother. Tate had wanted to ride in that ambulance, but he was concerned about Edie driving. In his truck, on the way there, Tate kept asking Edie what happened to his mother. She repeated much of the same story to him. They were sitting at the table, talking, and drinking coffee. Edie was not ready to tell Tate that the woman in the kitchen was emotionally unstable. She had been unkind to Edie with her remarks, and she had obviously sunken into a depression from her grief. Depression was another word the paramedics had mentioned in the kitchen. Neither Tate nor Edie knew what *respiratory depression* meant or why the paramedics had asked if Mrs. Ryman had taken any kind of medication.

"What happened after Ma passed out?" Tate asked Edie quietly in the waiting room which was about half full of people.

"I heard the paramedics say her breathing was shallow," Edie answered him. "I don't understand all of that medical lingo and I really think they use it in front of us on purpose, because if we knew what they were really saying, we would panic even more."

"I am panicked regardless," Tate told her. "I just lost my Pops. I can't go through this again." Edie touched Tate's leg and told him not to think like that. *Just wait and see what the doctor says. Hopefully we will know something soon.*

An hour later, Tate and Edie were called into a private office. A nurse escorted them into the room to meet with a doctor who wanted to discuss Mrs. Ryman's condition. For Tate, this felt dire. He recalled the last time, when it was Edie lying in a hospital bed, how he was brought directly to her room to see her. It had not been good news that she was in a coma, but she had been expected to recover – and she did. Tate was grateful to have Edie by his side now. He was tired of facing health emergencies. His father's illness for more than a year before his death had left him emotionally spent. He just wanted to resume some sort of normalcy in his life again. He was looking to do just that before Edie was in the car accident.

He had wanted to make her his wife.

After the doctor told them both to have a seat in the two chairs, side by side, in front of his desk, he also sat down on the opposite end of the desk. This doctor could have passed for a resident, he was very young, but Tate chose to trust what he had to say about his mother. Tate was not a man to judge.

Tate wanted to blurt out *how is she? Will my mother be okay?* But, he politely waited for the doctor to speak first.

"Your mother," the doctor looked at both Tate and Edie, and then back at Tate. "wasn't breathing regularly when the paramedics reached the scene. A short time later, in the ambulance, her heart stopped." Tate swallowed hard and Edie sat beside him, holding her breath, waiting for this to turn around to positive news. "She slipped into a coma afterward."

"But she's expected to recover, right?" Tate asked. "I mean, what exactly happened to her today? She's always been very healthy. She's never even been on prescription medicine in her entire life."

"That's where we are puzzled," the doctor interjected. "All of the signs, and very alarming symptoms immediately alerted us to an overdose. We found excessive amounts of opioid in her system."

"What's that?" Tate asked.

"It's a painkiller," the doctor replied.

Edie's mind raced. Mrs. Ryman was ready to give up today. And she obviously had. She tried to kill herself with Edie present. It made absolutely no sense. Why had she even wanted

Edie there? She was the one who summoned her, and had not been the most welcoming to her in that kitchen today.

"I am so confused," Tate spoke, as he looked at Edie beside him. "She has to wake up soon so she can clear up all of this craziness for us."

"What we do know is that your mother overdosed. Her stomach was pumped to save her life, but she did suffer some serious complications to her health. Heart damage for sure. We will be running further tests once she emerges from the coma."

Tate still had more questions, but the doctor was not the one he wanted to ask. It was Edie.

When they were alone again, waiting to be told they could see his mother, Tate paced the floor in a private waiting room as Edie sat down and watched him.

"Word for word. I want to know everything you and Ma talked about today. We both knew how strange it was when she asked you to come over. The two of you have never had a conversation beyond the weather and who knows what the hell else! Only one of us knows what my mother wanted today." Tate stopped walking around the room and he stood facing Edie, and she looked up at him.

"She was very hostile to me at times…" Edie carefully began. "I've never been the woman she wanted for you. She told me so. And, then, all the while she was talking, I could see signs. She was sad, maybe even depressed. Grief can be like a quicksand and I think your mother was sinking deeper and not able to pull herself out."

"They were together for fifty years," Tate defended his mother. "Of course she's sad and feeling hopeless."

"That's what I thought too," Edie agreed with him, "but then she asked me to help her die."

"What?" Tate's face fell. There was no way to prepare for the shock that rippled through his body.

"I know, I couldn't believe it either. I tried talking to her about how grief will make you think and feel things to the extreme, but she wouldn't hear of it. She chose me to help her end her life because she knows I'm familiar with grief and she also implied that it would be easy for me because I've never liked her."

"This is insane!" Tate was angry, and he was lashing out at Edie.

"Tell me about it. I was so close to running outside to get you, for help, but she stopped me. I know I shouldn't have Tate, but I thought it would have a reverse effect on her. I thought if she knew your father was okay, she would find a reason to go on…"

"Oh my God! You fucking told her about your dream!" Tate was livid.

"It wasn't a dream," Edie calmly defended herself, and then wished she hadn't. The look on Tate's face told her all she needed to know. He thought she was crazy. He had warned her to keep *that story* to herself. He didn't want to upset his mother as she grieved for his father. And, now, much worse happened. Tate would blame Edie for this for sure.

"What happened when you told her?" Tate asked. His jaw was clenched and his eyes could have pierced her.

"She didn't believe me at first because she said if her husband were to come back it would be to see her, not me. But, then, I told her he was sent to warn me about Sydney. It seemed like something clicked and she got it. She was not at all shocked that I said my sister tried to have me killed. And then she held her head and I could see she was not feeling well before she passed out."

"And you thought she passed out because of the shock you put her through?" Tate asked Edie.

"Yes, I did," Edie responded. "I had no idea she was taking drugs."

"My mother does not take drugs," Tate spoke adamantly.

"But, Tate, she said she wanted to die…" Edie attempted to convince him.

"Right, but how? And why did she need you there if she had already popped too damn many pills? And how did she even get her hands prescription medication?" Tate was so confused, but as he said those words, his eyes widened.

"Did you have your painkillers with you? Did you give my mother your meds?" His accusation was downright cruel, and not to mention outrageous.

"God, no!" Edie responded. "Who the hell do you think I am?"

"I don't know!" Tate screamed back. "This is all just too crazy and I'm trying to piece together something that makes sense."

"And it makes sense to believe that I would have aided your mother in overdosing?" Edie was the one angry now.

"No, of course not. I don't know what to think. I just know my mother, and what happened today does not add up." Tate turned away from Edie and walked over to the window. He stood in front of it, with his back to her, just as he had in the living room of their home when she told him what she experienced when she was comatose. When he couldn't face her, he didn't believe her. *If he could not trust her, how could they ever have a life together?*

"I need some air," Edie said, after they shared entirely too much silence. There was tension in the room and Tate never turned around from facing the window.

She walked outside in the cold wind and stood there, feeling sheer disbelief. What had brought her to this point? She had been so triumphant for so long at not letting pain get in the way. At fourteen, life's tragic circumstances had made her cold and even heartless. She learned to power through. She focused on success and money and her physical appearance. Those things fulfilled her. She was happy being who she was. Who she had taught herself and forced herself to be following a terrible tragedy that altered the course of her life. Edie didn't want to love anyone but herself. It was easier and painless that way. It somehow even worked when she met Tate. At first it had anyway. Now, things were changing.

With her hands in the pockets of her long winter white coat, she withstood the wind in her face for only a few more seconds before she reached in her handbag for her cell phone. She called for a taxi. There was a service in Dover, just ten minutes away. She wanted to go back to Mrs. Ryman's kitchen before the police labeled it a crime scene. Because if Tate blamed her, so would everyone else. It was time for Edie to look out for herself. No one else was going to.

Chapter 16

Tate was alone in that private waiting room. Any minute, he was hoping to be told that he could see his mother. He regretted chasing Edie away, but his confusion about what happened had led to anger. Still, he never should have accused the woman he loved of drugging his mother. That made about as much sense as his mother wanting to end her life. Nothing was adding up, and Tate sat there and allowed the stress of the last few weeks to consume him. He was bent forward on the chair with his elbows on his knees and his face in his hands. He wasn't near tears, but he felt terribly sad and alone.

When the nurse interrupted his thoughts, he stood up instantly. "Come with me," she told him. "Your mother is now in her own room, and you can see her."

Never in his entire life had Tate ever sat at the bedside of someone who was comatose. And now this was the second time in weeks. The two women he loved most in this world had dragged him through emotional hell as he sat beside their beds, wondering and waiting. First Edie, and now his mother.

She looked as if she was only sleeping. Unlike Edie, there were no wounds, no bandages to cover up any injury that had to heal. In a way, it was scarier this way for Tate. *What if there was damage he couldn't see? To his mother's heart? What if her brain had been deprived of oxygen for too long? What if he lost his mother so soon after his father's death?*

Tate had called his sister and she was going to book the first flight out from Florida. He didn't waste any time calling her. This was dire. Their mother was seventy-five years old and in a fragile state. She may have already given up. If what Edie said was true, she had wanted to die.

"Mom, really?" Tate spoke aloud because he knew she could hear him. Edie had confirmed that was possible. "This isn't you. You have to fight. What they are telling me does not add up. You've always had a zest for life that I've never seen in anyone else before. Come back to that. Come back to me…"

Mary Lou Ryman was walking on a path that led deep into the woods. There used to be a trail just like it behind her childhood home in Dover, where she would walk for what felt like miles. She recognized that same peaceful feeling again now, which she had not soaked up anywhere else in her life for many years. She was most definitely back there, relishing it, not having a care in the world. One foot in front of the other. Her inner peace increased with every step.

In the distance, far behind her, she thought she heard her son's voice, calling her *Ma*, summoning her back to him maybe? But, she only wanted to keep walking. She felt as if she never wanted to turn back. Her children were adults now and they no longer needed her. Her only two granddaughters, both on the verge of becoming teenagers, lived too far away. Twice a year visits were all she had to cherish. Rex, the love of her life, was gone. He was waiting for her, and she felt strongly about going to him now. *Maybe that was where this path led?*

Far down that path, as far as her eyes could take her, Mary Lou could see a man's stature. There were probably twenty or thirty trees between her and him, but she could see her husband leaning up against one. One leg bent behind him at the knee in his jeans and brown-tie shoes. His blue plaid shirt made that same color of blue in his eyes pop. She thought she had been so far away, but now she was right there, in front of him. She had not walked faster, nor had she run to him. She just saw him, wanted to be close to him, and then she instantly was.

"Lord have mercy…it's really you." Mary Lou reached out her hand and Rex did the same. His touch brought her back to life. She felt happy and whole again. Tears welled up in her eyes as he put his hand on the side of her face, cupping her cheek in the palm of his hand.

"My Lou," he said. "You need me."

"Yes, oh yes, I always have. I just cannot do this, not without you." Mary Lou hoped with all of her being that she was here to stay. Wherever this was, wherever he was, she wanted to be. For eternity.

Rex shook his head. "You need me to show you the way back," he began again. "You've lost your way, but you can't leave things how they are. You have to fix everything. That's our boy. He's in trouble. You never were a selfish woman, Lou. Don't allow your grief for me to change who you are."

"No…it already has. I can't face what I've done. Our son, he will be so disappointed in me. I could not bear that." Mary Lou was adamant. She was ashamed of her thoughts and her actions. Her actions that had backfired and almost took her life. She did feel relieved that she had not hurt Edie. She didn't think she had to explain any of this to Rex. And, yes, he already knew. The two of them stood together, embracing in a forest full of color, the breathtaking colors of autumn leaves filled every tree, near and far.

"Tate will suffer if you do not go back. Those girls are suffering. Someone has to make them, and everyone else, understand why their lives have come to this crazy crossroad. It's not too late to repair the damage."

"I tried to kill her, Rex," Mary Lou stated, just to clarify her unforgivable sin.

"So did her own sister. You, at least, see the harm in your actions now. Edie's sister does not. Edie's in danger, and you are the only one who can save her." Rex appeared worried, and Mary Lou wondered if he could already see the outcomes – both if she turned back, or if she chose not to.

"Our son will make it right," Mary Lou said, hoping her husband would agree.

"No. Our son, to a fault, has always seen only the good in everyone. He's blinded by his love for one woman and his trust for another. He needs guidance, or he will freefall. I know what you were just wondering, and I can answer that thought for you. I am unable to see the outcome if you go back. I just know to trust that if you do, everything will eventually be okay. What I can see, however, is the destructive path that our son will take in his life if you do not choose to go back and help him. A broken heart and severed trust will tear down the boy we raised, the man we were incredibly proud of. Go help him..."

Mary Lou stepped toward her husband. Her face was already wet with tears. He pulled her close, into his arms. Her senses were heightened. His touch. His scent. His handsome, masculine face and full head of wavy gray hair. The sound of his voice in her ears. It was all too much but she took every ounce of it in, consumed it all, as she knew this was goodbye again. She was still a mother. No matter the abundance of love she had for this man almost her entire life, she had to choose her son. He needed her more. Still, it pained Mary Lou to turn back.

"Please," she said to her husband as they parted and he smiled at her with such pride in his eyes. *His wife. Oh how he loved her. She was going to do the right thing.* "Please, do not let me cross back over to the other side feeling this bitter. I'm overwhelmed back there. You know that. I'm not myself anymore."

Rex took both of her hands in his. She felt something. Something more than before, more than she had ever felt in a lifetime of being with him. This was powerful beyond words. He had given her his strength and his goodness. She could feel it pulsing through her veins, with every beat of her heart. And she would take all of it with her. Before her eyes, his smile, his outer shell, all of him, slowly faded. And then disappeared. She was left standing there alone. But, she could still feel him. "Hold on to that," she heard the whisper of his voice. Mary Lou looked up high into the sky, far past the very tops of the trees that looked as if they reached the white puffy clouds in the clear blue sky. There were no tears in her eyes anymore. No sadness in her heart. And then she smiled.

Edie told the cab driver not to wait when he drove her up onto the driveway of Mrs. Ryman's house. She stepped out into the cold afternoon air, and walked on the sidewalk that Tate shoveled hours earlier. What a day this had turned out to be. When Edie woke up this morning, all she had wanted to do was confront her sister about the missing money in the Ryman's bank account. She was not going to allow Sydney to feed her the same ridiculous story that she told Tate. Sure, there may have been other accounts hacked at the bank, but the money shown as withdrawn from the Ryman's account was indeed gone. Edie was certain of it. And she knew Sydney was the culprit.

All of that craziness was still not far from her thoughts, but Edie forced herself to focus on why she wanted to be back at Tate's mother's house. She turned the knob of the outside door that led into the kitchen, and was not surprised to find it unlocked. Tate never locked the door to his mudroom either.

This time, Edie didn't bother to wipe off her wet boots on the rug inside of the door. She just charged into that kitchen and walked straight over to the trash basket which sat on the floor inside of the pantry. For a woman like Edie who was prim and proper, going through trash, especially someone else's, was enough to make her throw up. In this, case, however, she was on a mission. In the middle of coffee grounds and wadded up paper towels, Edie kept digging her hands deeper into that trash basket. She had never seen so many wadded up paper towels. And after a few more seconds of searching, it dawned on her. She took the time to unravel or shake out each wad of paper towels. After she did this three times, one of the wads felt heavier. Two shakes later and a pill bottle fell onto the heap of trash at the top of the basket.

Edie picked up the prescription pill bottle and read the label. It was the Vicodin in her name, prescribed just days ago. *Busted.* Mrs. Ryman had stolen Edie's pills. Edie had not brought them along in her purse, as Tate accused her of doing. His mother had to have been at their house, snooping with the intent to steal. Edie's mind was reeling. If Mrs. Ryman wanted to take her own life and had decided to overdose, it did make sense to steal medication from someone who had just been prescribed a painkiller. But, what baffled Edie beyond words was *why Mrs. Ryman wanted her help. Why did she request for her to be there?* None of that made sense.

With the empty pill bottle in her hands, Edie was still standing over the trash basket when the kitchen door opened without any warning.

"What are you doing here?" Edie was asked, frankly.

Edie had spent the last two and a half years of her life with this man, but right now the look she witnessed on Tate's face was foreign to her. Telling him that she just rooted through his mother's trash to find the empty pill bottle now in her hands was going to be the easy part. All she had to do was tell him the truth. The difficult, maybe even impossible, part was going to be having him believe her.

Chapter 17

"I found out that you took a cab from the hospital," Tate told her, as he closed the door behind him. "I don't know why, but I drove by here first. Why didn't you go home?"

"Why did you come here first?" she turned the question around to him. "I'll answer that for you. You had the same thought as I did. Your mother stole my prescription. I know that for sure now. I just found it in her trash." Edie held up the empty pill bottle for Tate to get a closer look.

"I didn't just walk in on you planting that in her trash?" Tate's question, even though she was partly expecting it, angered Edie.

"Do you even know who I am?" she asked him, trying not to sound angry but she most certainly was.

"I thought I did," he answered her honestly. "I also believe that I know my own mother very well. She would never attempt to take her own life."

"So this was premeditated murder on my part?" Edie's attitude was snarky. "And why would I want to kill your mother? You just lost your father for chrissakes!"

"Just help me to understand this," Tate begged.

"I'm the wrong person to ask," she replied. "I have just as many questions as you do. It's your mother who needs to fill in the blanks." After she spoke, Edie silently hoped Mrs. Ryman's condition had not taken a turn for the worse. Tate had left the hospital to look for her, so Edie assumed nothing terrible happened to his mother.

"Let's just hope she can," Tate added.

"Has her condition changed at all?" Edie asked, and she actually felt genuinely concerned.

"No," Tate shook his head.

"Are you going back there tonight?" she asked, referring to the hospital.

"Kathy's flight will be in late this afternoon. I want to be at the hospital when she gets there," Tate explained.

"You should be there now," Edie stated.

"I was worried about you," he admitted.

"I think you suspected me and that's why you are here," she told him, still feeling hurt by his distrust of her.

"Don't make me choose between you and my mother," he warned her.

"What does that even mean?" she put him on the spot. He did not answer her, so Edie came to her own painful conclusion. His mother meant more to him.

※

As soon as Tate dropped off Edie at home, he left again for the hospital. He never asked her if she wanted to go along with him, and she never said that she would have liked to either. The communication between them was again distant and tense, which was not unfamiliar territory for them. But, when his truck turned off of their lane road, Edie was already in the driver's seat of her own car. She could not just sit around the house by herself.

When she walked through the automatic door of Ry's Market, she felt odd. She never liked going in there. She wasn't at all domestic and absolutely hated to shop for groceries. Tate always did the shopping because for most of the two years they lived together, he was working at the market for his father. Edie preferred to shop at an organic store in Dover and did so often, during or after work.

She did not think anyone would recognize her, but she also had no idea where to find Sydney or the location of an office in that building. One of the cashiers caught her eye and at the moment she was not busy, so Edie walked up to the middle-aged woman with a French braid halfway down her back. She was wearing one of those burgundy Ry's Market smocks and Edie could have rolled her eyes. *Sydney's uniform, day in and day out.*

"Hi, can I bother you for a moment? I'm looking for Sydney Klein..." Edie was polite and the employee was as well when she directed her to the back of the store.

When Edie made her way through the market, she found the door, knocked twice, and walked in. The size of the room took her by surprise. She felt like if she reached her arms out as wide as she could, she may have been able to touch all four walls. Close corners, for sure. Then her sister spun around in her chair in front of a laptop computer on an incredibly small desk.

"Edie? What are you doing here?" Edie expected her reaction. Really, the two of them, no matter where they were, were never pleased to see each other.

"Well I obviously came to see you," Edie replied in her typical sarcastic tone.

"There's a folding chair against the wall if you need to sit," Sydney offered, but she never got up to get it for her.

"I'll stand," Edie replied. "And I'll also get right to the point of why I'm here." Sydney sized up her sister standing before her, looking like a model right out of a magazine. Her black leggings hugged her every curve, her high boots were stylish and the color of her fitted winter white sweater complimented her long, shiny blonde hair. Edie had left her coat in the car, and she was happy she had because that small windowless office was stuffy.

"I know that Tate believed your bullshit excuse about the bank," Edie began, and Sydney never flinched but she did feel her own heart beat quicken. *Was Edie onto her?* "What did you do with the fifty grand, Syd?"

Sydney rolled her eyes. "It really doesn't matter what you think. Tate believes me. These things happen when you're dealing with millions of dollars."

Edie scoffed. "No, these things only happen when you put an inexperienced moron in charge." Edie also wanted to call her a thief.

"If you came here to insult me, you can leave," Sydney told her in no uncertain terms.

"Oh, I'm far from ready to leave," Edie responded. She paced back and forth in front of Sydney before she spoke again. The closer she got enabled Sydney to see how the bruise on her forehead was still very prominent, even concealed underneath makeup.

"I have work to do, you know how that is," Sydney barked at her.

"Actually, right now, I'm on a leave from my job. I had an accident that currently is preventing me from living my life." Edie glared at her sister.

"You're lucky to be alive, sis." That comment sent chills through Edie.

"Yes I am," she agreed, "but if you would have had your way, or a little more luck on your side, I wouldn't be." Edie left it at that, and then waited for Sydney to respond.

"You're talking out of your head…must be the repercussions of that nasty bump that your Rodan + Fields is failing to cover up." Sydney was far from being sympathetic, and Edie could have hauled off and slapped her.

"Speaking of out of my head, or out of my body," Edie said in a matter-of-fact tone, "I had one of *those* crazy experiences the night of my accident." Sydney instantly looked confused, but listened raptly. "I watched the paramedics at the accident scene. I was actually out of my body. Just like in the movies. I thought I had died, but someone was sent for me, to help me make sense of what happened."

"Are you okay?" Sydney interrupted, feeling freaked out. "Does Tate know you're here?"

"I'm pretty clear-headed right now, if that's what you are asking. And, I'm a big girl. I don't need Tate to hold my hand." Edie was going all the way with this. She wanted her sister to know everything. "As I was saying… Rex Ryman was sent to me that night."

"You saw a dead man?" Sydney interjected with wide eyes.

"I did, and I also saw you. Right here. In this office. And in the parking lot." Edie's words caused confusion and sheer panic for Sydney. *That was not possible.* "So, I witnessed your interaction with the thug who wanted to be paid for a job you told him he had not finished. I would say fifty grand from the market's account came in handy for you to pay off your hitman."

Sydney laughed out loud. It was a nervous laugh, which Edie recognized. "You are fucking insane, big sister! Does Tate know you are talking like this?"

"Stop bringing Tate into this," Edie insisted. "No, wait. He's the reason, isn't he? You're obsessed with the man I–"

"The man you what, sis? Live with? Are sleeping with? The man you call your boyfriend like if you're still in high school? Try saying it, Edie." Sydney waited, but not long enough for Edie to respond before she spoke again. "You can't say it because you are incapable of feeling it. It's called love. And Tate deserves it. He deserves so much more than you can give him!" Sydney had raised her voice with a truth she had believed for years now.

"What Tate and I share is none of your business," Edie stated. "You need to get a life of your own and leave us alone."

"Is that what you came here to tell me today?" Sydney pushed her.

"That, and I just wanted to prepare you for a visit from law enforcement. They come after people like you who break the law. Oh, and I'm not holding back when I turn you in. They can lock you up for all I care!"

"Of course they will believe you...your story isn't the least bit crazy." Sydney mocked her.

"I can prove the money is missing, and I'm sure they can track a thug suddenly paying off bills or wildly spending an awful lot of money everywhere." Edie was proud of herself. The story that Tate was so afraid of everyone else knowing, especially his mother, didn't even have to come out in its entirety in order for Sydney to pay. Her sister could very well go to prison, and Edie didn't even care. All she could think about was she had almost died and it was this person's doing. This person sitting in front of her now, who was her only family left in this world. *But had she ever really cared about claiming her? No, and she most certainly didn't give a damn now either.*

"You may want to wait on going to the police," Sydney spoke calmly. "You know, like the old saying goes, if you scratch my back, I'll scratch yours?" Edie frowned at Sydney. She was more than confused. Until Sydney clarified it all for her. "If Mrs. Ryman dies, you will be the one rotting in a jail cell." Edie was surprised that Sydney already knew about Mrs. Ryman's overdose that occurred merely hours earlier.

"I had nothing to do with that," Edie defended herself.

"Oh but it will not look like that at all," Sydney spoke with certainty, a confidence that Edie barely recognized in her. "It was the perfect plan, don't you think? I mean, right up until the little old lady mixed up her coffee with the cup meant for you."

Chapter 18

After Tate spoke with his sister outside of their mother's hospital room, they sat together at her bedside, waiting and willing her to wake up. To come back to her family. All of his life, Tate listened and always sought advice from his sister, ten years older and wiser than him. He could not get out of his mind what she said to him after he tried to explain the overdose story. When he stated that their mother had somehow ended up with Edie's drugs in her system, his sister's exact words were, *It's time for you to open your eyes, little brother. Do not trust Edie Klein.*

Edie took three steps backward in that stuffy little office. She felt her body bump up against the closed door. She just stood there, feeling like she could not get enough air to breathe. This was all so unbelievable, and shocking. If what Sydney said were true, Tate's mother had tried to kill her too. That was the missing link. Mary Lou Ryman had not wanted to take her own life. She had stolen Edie's pain medicine, summoned her to the house, poured her a tainted cup of coffee, and had planned to make it look as if Edie was suicidal. *But why?* Because she was a grief-stricken woman who had gone to extremes to protect her son from a woman she did not approve of? *But, to resort to murder?* Nothing made sense to Edie anymore. Except for the fact that she was surrounded by recklessness. And she was not safe. She had never before been this scared out of her mind.

With one arm behind her back, Edie reached for the doorknob. Sydney had not moved. She only continued to sit there and wait for Edie's reaction. Which was, for Edie to run.

She opened the door behind her back, and took off running through the aisles of Ry's Market. She just missed knocking over a child around one corner, and actually did have a collision with the front end of a woman's grocery cart. It was when Edie was in aisle three, almost to the front entrance of the store, that she heard someone speak loudly to her.

"She's dangerous," were the words coming from a petite old man, sitting on a red milk crate on the floor in front of a few partially stocked shelves, and he was wearing one of those god-awful burgundy smocks.

Edie came to a halt, and looked back at him. "Who is?"

"Our new store manager…" he told her, and Edie took a few steps closer to him. "I'm Tommy Kampwerth, I was a good friend of Rex's, and his wife. I should have done more to protect her."

"What are you saying?" Edie glanced far down their aisle, hoping Sydney had not followed her.

"My grandson –he's our bank president in this town– wanted to go to the police, but Lou said she would handle it. Well look where handling it got her. She's in a hospital bed, unconscious." Tommy shook his head solemnly, as he remained seated on that crate on the floor.

"So you think your new store manager is the one responsible for Mrs. Ryman's condition?" Edie asked, wondering if this elderly man, so loyal to the Rymans, knew who she was. Her connection to Tate, and especially to Sydney.

"I don't trust her," he replied.

※

Trust. Tate trusted that the scaffolding would hold him at every construction site where he worked off the ground, multiple floors and many stories high. He never saw the need to wear a harness. He trusted he would not fall. With Edie, he had trusted and loved her, but he now believed she had failed him.

Six months after his mother's overdose, which Tate was certain Edie played a role in somehow, Mary Lou remained comatose. Her daughter, Kathy traveled to Camden every weekend to sit by her bedside at the nursing home where Mary Lou was transferred after a one-month hospital stay. Tate spent every evening sitting alongside his mother's bedside for hours on end. During the day, he was working in construction again. It was the only thing that fulfilled him in his life now.

Edie had been a suspect in the Camden Police Department's investigation into Mrs. Ryman's overdose. Tate's sister, Kathy had made sure of that. The case, however, was left open-ended as there was no proof for how Mrs. Ryman actually got a hold of the prescription drugs. *Were the drugs dissolved in the coffee she drank because she had crushed the entire bottle of opioids herself when grief consumed her and she opted to end her own life? Or had someone else premeditated her murder?* Edie was a free woman in more ways than one.

It had also been six months since Edie moved out of Tate's house and into a high-rise apartment in Dover, not too many blocks away from Stockmann Advertising. Sitting in her office now, Edie rose from her chair to stretch her long legs. She had been focused on her computer for hours. Work was her constant, more than ever in her life now. She smoothed the wrinkles from the short skirt of her peach business suit with her hands. Her bone-colored booties had three-inch heels on them and she pointed the toes of them in front of her, one and then the other, until she reached the window that spanned more than half of the wall in her ninth floor office. There was construction carrying on across the way, and her mind went to him. It always did. She had heard Tate resumed his career in construction, and that made her happy for him. She knew how much he needed to be in that element, working with his hands. She admired how if he could dream it in his creative mind, he could put his hands to work and watch that visual come to life. There was so much she had not appreciated about him then, but she did now. Now that it was too late.

A sunbeam through another window went unnoticed on this summer day. This was a mental institution in Dover where every window was barred, spoiling much of the peace and the beauty of peering out of it. Those feelings had been lost to Sydney anyway. Sydney shared her room with a woman who was said to have gone out of her mind more than twenty years ago after her husband died a heroic death as a fireman at the site of the World Trade Center on 9-11. Someone had mentioned Sydney's roommate being the mother of Jack the Bartender at Lantern Inn in Camden. Sydney never asked her roomie any questions. In fact, she had never even heard her speak. Just in her sleep, once in awhile, when she would cry, too. That was what her life had come to. Lying in parallel twin beds with a crazy woman. Locked in an institution because prison time for her crimes had not deemed fitting. Sydney had done more than steal thousands of dollars to hire a hitman. She had obsessed over a man and intended to hurt the one who got in her way. Her own sister.

When Edie gave her statement to the police, and then later to the psychiatrist assigned to evaluate Sydney, she spoke of her sister as *crazy*. She embellished more than a few stories pertaining to their childhood after their parents had been killed. *Sydney, the introvert, had obsessive and strange behaviors,* she used to scare me, and repeatedly threatened my life, Edie had stated because she wanted Sydney out of her life, locked up for the rest of hers. And Edie ensured that it happened. Sydney was sentenced for eighteen months. Reevaluation would occur after her time was served.

That was the final straw for Tate. He could not fathom anyone turning on their next of kin. He also could not handle being deceived by both sisters. He had loved them both in completely different ways. And then he wanted both of them out of his life. He blamed Sydney for taking advantage of him, his family's business, and his mother. And he blamed Edie for her downfall. Pushing a person away, time and again, eventually does them in. Sydney may have gone over the edge, but Tate believed it was Edie who coerced her. Most of all, the pain that would not subside for Tate, was seeing his mother in an unresponsive state, day after day, week after week, and for months on end. Tate blamed Edie for his mother's lifelessness, and believed he always would.

Chapter 19

Tate passed Ry's Market on his way home from the construction site. It was ninety-two degrees and he was driving with his truck windows down. He stopped at the market at least three times a week, just to check on things. The only thing he had not handed over control of yet to the new store manager were the books. Tate handled payroll and oversaw all of the ins and outs. The new store manager was a fifty-two-year-old man who came with previous management experience after having spent more than twenty years in the grocer business in various cities across Delaware. Tate knew his mother would have labeled the man as a big wig in their little town's market, but he was confident with his decision. As long as the market was in their mother's name, Tate and Kathy could not sell the business. Both were relieved that their hands were indeed tied, especially Tate, because selling the business would mean the end of their parents' legacy. The two of them continued to have high hopes for their mother to wake up and regain her life. If she did not, the market was willed to Rex and Lou's children.

He walked in through the automatic door and began to make his way down aisle three, en route to the office. As soon as he stepped foot on the large green and white tiled floor, in that direction, Tate knew he had made a mistake if he thought he was in hurry. There, seated on that red milk crate, still stocking shelves for the day, was Tommy Kampwerth. He stopped Tate to talk at least once a week.

"Hiya Tommy," Tate spoke first, because it was the polite thing to do instead of just walking by when Tommy wasn't looking.

"Tate, my boy, how are you?" Tommy's word choice always made Tate miss his father. His mother, too, for that matter.

"Doing good, how are you?" Tate stopped walking when he reached the crate, where Tommy remained seated and looked up at him.

"I've been okay," he answered. "Just living every day." After a pause, Tommy asked what he always did. "How's your Ma? I need to stop by the home to see her again soon."

"No change," Tate replied, and sadly he had gotten used to saying those words.

"She'll open those baby blues when she's ready," Tommy told Tate.

"I know," he replied, nodding his head.

"In the meantime, you know your Ma would want you to go on. Live happily. Don't hold grudges. They're no good. Only good for eating away at your soul." Tate knew what Tommy meant. It wasn't the first time in the last six months that he had brought up Edie. Lots of people still spoke her name. No one could seem to think of one without the other. Still, Tate wished they all would just let him forget. If that were possible.

"I hear ya, man. Don't you worry...I've got his life thing figured out. And, believe me, some things just aren't worth the pain." Tate patted Tommy on the shoulder and he started to walk away.

"And sometimes," Tommy called after him, "pain won't go away until you face it." Tate left him with a wave of his hand in the air behind him.

* * *

"Okay, Ma...don't you think six months, and counting, is a long enough damn time?" Tate asked, as he sat down alongside of his mother's bed and took her hand in his. "I mean, really, you need to make yourself useful. Cook me a meal, bake me some of those turtle brownies, or have a cup of coffee with me..." Tate caught himself after he said those words. *A cup of coffee.* He sighed, and then spoke again.

"What the hell happened that day, Ma? You need to wake up and fill me in. My life's been quite the mess because of it. I did what I had to do, what I felt like I needed to do, but I can't stop thinking...and hurting. Will you please help me? I'm giving you a purpose here. I need my Ma."

It was dark and Mary Lou was tired. Tired of trying to squeeze the hand that held hers at her bedside. Worn down from failed efforts to lift her eyelids at the sound of her name from the lips of one of her two children, or her two granddaughters who had come to see her a few times. *If she wanted to go back, why had she not been able to wake up and return to her life?* Maybe, she was afraid to admit it to herself. She was waiting for the one person who had not yet come to visit her.

Tate caught himself nodding off. It was after ten o'clock, and he had already spent four hours with his mother again. He touched his mother's hand one last time. "See you tomorrow night, Ma. I'm not going to stop pushing you, and nagging you to wake up. I need you." In the dark room, Tate took two steps away from the bed when he felt compelled to look back. He thought he heard something, but it could have been like all of the other times when he had willed her to wake up. It was wishful thinking to believe he saw her mouth twitch, or her eyes flutter. This time, however, it was not a movement that he saw. It was something he had heard.

Tate stared in the dark at his mother's still body. Her white hair made her look so angelic. Her body was covered up to her waist, her arms outside of the blanket. It was dark in there, and other than her hair, he could only see her form in the bed. He turned back toward the door. It was late. He was tired. *And how many times hadn't he thought this was it. She was going to wake up.*

"E…"

Tate stopped. And he immediately turned around. His eyes were wide, and from what he could see, his mother's eyes were still closed. But her mouth...her lips...were attempting to move. "Ma!" Tate raced over to her and placed his own face just inches from hers. Her eyelids fluttered and more sound came from her mouth. "E...D"

"Edie? Ma, it's me Tate. Edie is not here."

"Her...See h..e..r." Tate knew what he heard.

"It's okay, it's all good. You're back. I need to get a nurse, get you checked out by a doctor. Oh, thank God, you're back. You're talking. You know who I am." Tate spoke one thing after another as he watched his mother completely open her eyes.

"Get... E...D." Tate's mother was persistent.

"Yes, I will. I will." Tate wanted to know why. He also fretted about the six months that had passed. They were no longer a couple, no longer in each other's lives. They weren't even speaking. Their lives had gone on without each other. Tate assumed Edie was dating. A woman like her was never alone for long. She was beautiful. She was all he still thought about, but he knew, for him, she just wasn't meant to be. And now his mother wanted him to bring her back. He had to. They all had unanswered questions. Tate just hoped he could handle seeing Edie Klein again.

Tate never left his mother's side all night long. The nurses kept coming into her room to check on her, talk to her, and everyone was in complete awe that after six months this woman was awake, coherent, and even adamant about seeing a woman named Edie.

It was five o'clock in the morning when Mary Lou sat up in her bed, and called out Tate's name. He had dozed off for awhile in the chair beside her. "It's morning," she said to him as he peeled his eyes open and tried to smile at her.

"Barely, Ma," he said, still smiling.

"Go get her... for me." Her speech had already improved from slow and choppy syllables to just slurred words. The doctor would be there to examine her today. Tate already knew her brain was fine. She knew him. She remembered her life. She could speak, comprehend. He now hoped her heart would be unaffected from the overdose as well.

"I know how important seeing Edie is to you," Tate began. "It's all you've been talking about, and asking for. But, Ma, we all have questions. Can't you just talk to me? Tell me what happened, first. And then, if you still need to talk to Edie, maybe I'll understand why."

"So ash-am-ed," Mary Lou responded. "I can't. Not until...I...see...E...D." Tate saw the tears well up in her eyes, and he stopped pushing.

"I'll get her. I'll bring her to you." Tate stood up, kissed his mother on the forehead. He looked back at her one more time before he left the room at the nursing home. It had been six long months. It was unreal how this had finally happened.

Chapter 20

Tate went home. He took a shower, shaved his face, and dressed again in faded denim and a navy blue t-shirt. It was fitted and formed over his biceps and on his abs. The curls in his hair were still wet when he made his way to the mudroom and sat down on the second step to put on his boots. *Should he call first? Text, so he would not have to actually talk to her?* He knew where her new apartment building was located in Dover. *Maybe he would just drive there? But what would he say when he saw her? What if she wasn't alone?*

He nearly drove himself crazy with his own thoughts. He stood up abruptly from the step. His boots were laced and it was time to go. He got into his truck and drove to Dover.

He left the engine running and the air conditioning on high. It was barely seven o'clock in the morning and already almost ninety degrees outside. Tate was in the parking lot of the apartment complex where Edie now lived. He remembered how she had spoken about living in a *house* with him. She had previously lived in apartments and complained about the space, the neighbors on the other side of the walls. This was a ritzy complex, Tate had to admit, but he knew how Edie liked her space. There was a time when he wanted nothing more than to share his space with her.

Her car was still in the parking lot, so Tate decided to wait until she came out of the apartment building to leave for work. He was relieved she had not left already, but knowing her, he knew it would be soon.

Ten minutes passed and then he saw the doorman open the main door for a woman. She wore a black skirt, above the knees and with a kick pleat on the side, and a sleeveless sheer white button-down blouse with a tall collar. Her red heels were high. Her briefcase, gripped tightly, swung back and forth from her hand. Her hair was in a high bun. She wore her dark-rimmed glasses today. Her contacts must have been giving her trouble again as Tate knew she rarely left the house wearing her glasses. He vividly remembered her wearing those glasses at night, sitting up in bed, with her laptop on the duvet in front of her. He remembered it all. Everything about this woman.

He killed the engine of his truck and got out. His boots hit the pavement and picked up pace. She was already opening her car door to get inside. The doorman remained outside of the building and had his eyes on the man in the parking lot, approaching Edie.

Edie was looking down, readying to put her briefcase onto the seat first, when Tate spoke as he reached the back bumper of her car. "Edie…"

She had heard him say her name thousands of times before. His voice, she always loved the way it sounded, especially when her name rolled off of his tongue. Deep and masculine, yet always gentle. She used to think about how his voice would be perfect to sing a baby to sleep. But she wasn't allowed to have those thoughts anymore. It wasn't good for anyone, especially not for her to dwell on what might have been. She had messed that up for them. There was no way to conceal the surprise on her face. She looked up, she stared, and then she forced herself to speak. "Tate…What are you doing here?" Edie immediately thought of his mother. She had been praying consistently for her recovery, and Edie had not prayed to a God since she was fourteen years old.

Tate stepped closer to her. She could smell how he was fresh out of the shower, his wet hair gave way to that as well.

"I'm sorry…I didn't mean to startle you, or catch you off guard." Tate didn't know what else to say to her. He knew he just needed to say why he came. *Get to the point. Stop staring. Stop feeling.*

"Oh, it's okay. I'm just going to work." She wanted to say she had a meeting in fifteen minutes, but she was afraid she would rush him away. It just felt really nice to see him again. To be in this moment.

"Right, and I won't keep you. I, um, have some news," Tate looked down at his feet for a moment. His mother. She was the reason they had fallen apart. The reason he had told her it was over, and he wanted her out of his house, out of his life. Those were words of anger, spoken at a time when he was scared. Scared for his mother's life. Fearful of what had happened to her. He still had no answers, but so much time had gone by and he no longer felt those awful feelings for her. He recognized what this was. No matter what had happened, he was a man who knew how to forgive. And, somehow, he believed it was his mother who would need the forgiveness now. It was how she had looked at him when she asked for Edie. And she had spoken the word, *ashamed*. "It's Ma," he finally said. "She's awake."

"Oh thank God!" Edie immediately reacted with those words, and Tate thought to himself how he had not remembered her ever saying that before. "Is she okay? Does there seem to be any health issues as the doctor originally thought?"

"Her doctor will see her today, but she knows what's what and can talk, slowly but clearly." Tate was happy to share that good news with Edie. Other than a phone call to his sister in Florida, Edie was the only other person he had told.

"Wonderful. I'm truly happy for you, and her," Edie smiled, and then she glanced away. It was just too hard to look at him and remember. He loved her. And then he had some terribly harsh words for her, and had hurt her. "And, Tate," she added, "thank you for coming to share the good news with me. It means a lot to me." Edie acted as if she was giving him her parting words, and Tate spoke up quickly.

"She's asking for you," he told her outright.

"Me? I don't think that's a very good idea…" Edie was equally as curious as he was to find out what his mother wanted, but she didn't want to upset anyone by showing up where she did not feel welcome.

"She wants you there, E." Just to hear him call her that again had stirred her. She quickly reminded herself how Tate was there on behalf of his mother. That was all it was. Letting go of this man had been one of the hardest things she ever was forced to do. Every passing day and night, every baby step in the opposite direction from him had been progress for her. She could not and would not allow herself to go back. She knew she was strong, but she also knew what had come very close to breaking her.

"I'm sorry, Tate. I don't know if I can go to her. I mean, we've been through this. I know you and Kathy believed I put your mother in that terrible medical state, but I know I did not. I know she was the dangerous one that day, a risk to me and to herself. I guess what I'm trying to say is, I already have all the answers I need. I do feel happy for you and your family, knowing you have your Ma back."

"You can't do this," he told her, looking defeated. "She woke up late last night, and her first word was your name. She's unable to relax her mind. She needs to speak with you, and she will not tell me why. Edie, please, if anything, she needs peace - and I know I need closure."

The word closure came out of his mouth by surprise to him. He didn't know if he meant it or not. And Edie suspected he did. Maybe that's what this was about? *Tying up a terribly loose end. Finding a way to make peace in order to heal and move on.*

"Alright. I have a meeting in just minutes," she began to explain, and Tate suddenly was reminded how career driven she was. Edie, the successful account executive always emerged and was put first and foremost. He felt a familiar pang of resentment. "I will call to reschedule it on my way to see your mother," she told him, and caught him by surprise.

"You will?" he asked her.

"Tate, she's been asleep for too long. If she feels as strongly as you say she does about wanting to see me, then I can't put her off. I'll call it an emergency with a family friend," she explained, and Tate wanted to tell her she was more than a family friend, but he couldn't. For one, his family never welcomed her, never treated her like they should have. Well, maybe his father had more than any one of them. And he also had lost his right to call her anything at all.

"I can drive you?" Tate offered.

"No, thank you. I'd like to have my car there." Edie was being honest. She was an independent woman, and even Tate could never change that about her. He knew that all too well.

"I understand. It's the nursing home, three blocks south of Bayhealth," he instructed her.

"Okay, thank you."

"No, Edie. Thank you." Tate smiled sincerely, took one step toward her, and then stopped himself. He turned then, and walked back to his truck as she got into her own car. He would see her in a little while.

Chapter 21

Tate was waiting for her when she pulled up to the nursing home building. She noticed that he had just parked underneath a large overhang, so she drove up behind him there. Both of them ignored the pickup and drop-off, fifteen minute maximum sign that was posted.

Edie allowed Tate to hold the door for her and once she stepped inside the carpeted lobby, the scent overwhelmed her. It took her back to when she was fourteen years old and had spent time in both a hospital and a funeral home, following the accident and her parents' deaths. The scent that hung in the air now was a cross between both of those awful places that only held the saddest, emptiest memories.

"You okay?" Tate asked her, and Edie was instantly reminded how he could sometimes read her so well. She missed that. Her life was quite lonely now.

"Yes, I'm fine. It's just the smell in here," she kept her voice down.

"I guess I'm immune to it after all this time," he stated, and shook his head. *How nice it was going to be to get his mother out of this place. And soon.*

They walked in silence through the lobby, and down a long corridor. Edie had never before in her life seen so many wheelchairs, slumped bodies, wild bedheads of thin white hair, and sad, lost faces. She walked in sync with Tate and he had read her mind. *Just get her to where we are going. She can't take a place like this. She never will have the gift of watching her parents grow old.*

When they reached the door to Mrs. Ryman's room, Tate stepped back for Edie to go in first. "No, you go first," she told him. She was terrified of this moment, and had not allowed herself to really dwell on that fear until just now.

"It's going to be okay," he tried to reassure her.

"Easy for you to say," she replied, halfheartedly, and he chuckled. *What else could he do at this point?* Their life together was gone, and if he dwelled on that, he easily would have gotten lost in regret.

When Tate walked into the room first, Edie stayed behind him. In her heels, she was almost the same height as him. She moved her body from his guard, and looked directly at the bed in the room. Mrs. Ryman was sitting up in it. Her white hair was fixed in its trademark bob, her pink nightgown looked fresh and crisp as if someone had ironed it. And the expression on her face was one that Edie could not quite read. She wore no smile, and her eyes looked sad – or quite possibly remorseful.

"Ma, look who I brought for you," Tate spoke, carefully. There was no love lost between the two women in this room. One, however, wanted to see the other so badly that Tate had swallowed his pride and granted her wish.

"Come, please, sit." Her words were slow, but Edie understood them. Tate stepped back for Edie, and that's when his mother asked him to leave.

"You want me to go? No. I have a right to stay. Ma, I have questions, too." Tate almost sounded as if he was ten years old again, and he held his breath as he awaited permission to stay in the room. To learn the truth. Finally.

"I wish to speak…to…her…alone." His mother's speech slowed, and Tate recognized how his defiance had affected her.

He muttered, *for chrissakes. I'll be close by.* And then he left the room, closing the door not so quietly behind him.

Suddenly Edie, who was still standing far enough away to bolt out of the door if she had to, felt edgier without Tate present in the room with them.

"Sit, please…" Mrs. Ryman reminded her.

"I can't help but remember the last time you told me to have a seat," Edie spoke forwardly and then slowly made her way over to the chair. Mrs. Ryman's response was silence. She placed both of her hands on her lap and momentarily closed her eyes. Little did Edie know that she was asking her husband to send her strength. Strength to admit she was terribly wrong.

"I lied to you..." Mrs. Ryman began, once she opened her eyes again and looked directly at Edie, sitting on the edge of the chair. She could not relax there. "And I was wrong. So wrong." She was slow to string her words together, and Edie almost could not believe her ears. She, of course, knew her own innocence, but to hear a woman like the proper, do-no-wrong Mary Lou Ryman admit her guilt was almost unbelievable. This entire mess was astonishing. And this was what Edie's life had come to. Her sister, who wanted her dead, was in a mental institution. And a woman, who could have become her mother-in-law one day, had also premeditated murdering her.

"I had no right to judge you, and that's all I ever did. I don't know how I will face my son from this day forward. I can only hope you will find it in your heart to forgive me one day. His love for you will allow him to try to forgive me, I do know that. I don't expect you to understand. I don't even understand. I was consumed in my grief, but that is no excuse." Edie sat silently, listening but not always looking at Mrs. Ryman. Her legs were crossed and her one red heel digging into the carpet was easier to focus on right now. She had heard every word that Mrs. Ryman was saying to her, but the part about Tate's love for her echoed in her ears. A lot had happened in six months.

"I stole your medication. I crushed all those pills and put them into one coffee mug. My intent was for you to drink it," Mrs. Ryman admitted, and Edie noticed her folded hands on her lap were shaking profusely. "I'm an old fool. I got what I deserved, maybe you think the repercussions should have been harsher." Edie looked directly at her now. She saw the tears welling up in her eyes. As strange as it felt, Edie actually admired this woman in front of her right now. She had a high regard for a woman who was strong enough to allow herself to cry. Unshed tears had become Edie's forte in life.

Mrs. Ryman paused to cry. She sat there silently sobbing. If Edie had not been looking at her, she would never have seen her pain, nor the tears flooding her cheeks, one after another.

Edie couldn't bring herself to say anything, and she didn't know what else to do. She only chose to act before she lost her courage. She had never touched this woman before. Never wanted to get close enough to. Edie stood from her chair, walked to the edge of the bed, and placed both of her hands on overtop of Mrs. Ryman's. She could feel the wrinkles, the feebleness to the bones. Slowly, Mrs. Ryman's hands had ceased to tremble. "Thank you," she whispered to Edie, her face tear soaked. And Edie leaned in closer and enveloped this petite, aging woman into her arms. There was a peace in both of their hearts at this moment that neither one of them could explain or wanted to speak of. They just relished the feeling all around.

The door, which Tate had closed in somewhat of a huff when he was told to leave earlier, was now cracked just enough for him to see and hear. And he had witnessed, from the hallway, all that he needed to know. Edie may have been too strong to cry, but Tate wasn't. He stood there, consumed with emotion as he peered through that slightly opened door, never loving either one of those two women more. What a crazy way to realize that he was one blessed man.

Tate was in the hallway, standing just a few feet from the door, when Edie stepped out. "Hi," he said to her first. He was unsure at this point if he would tell her or even his mother that he had overheard them. And that he knew the truth now.

She softly smiled at him, but did not speak. Her tears that were fighting to freefall still remained unshed. It's just what Edie did. It's how she rolled now for most of her life. What happened in there with Tate's mother, all of it, was just so difficult. Edie wanted to forgive her, to give her the peace she so obviously needed. In the midst of doing the noble thing, Edie also realized just how much she cared about Mrs. Ryman. It was unexplainable to feel anything for her, but she did. And now she wanted to run. It was time to get back to her life, and her life alone. There was just too much pain when she allowed anyone to get too close.

"How did it go in there?" Tate asked her, and she could see the genuine concern he had for her. That was another reason why she needed to run.

"It's all going to be okay. Your mother can move on now, with peace in her heart, I hope." Edie meant those words.

"I can't pretend I didn't listen in," he admitted, walking over to her side of the hallway.

"A cracked door is so lame," she teased him, to lighten the mood.

He laughed, and then stood close to her. "Walk outside with me. I don't want to be overheard in here." Edie nodded her head. She really just wanted to leave there and never look back.

When they reached the outdoors, the temperature difference instantly had gone from cool air conditioning to hot, humid air blowing in their faces, and almost instantly leaving their skin with a sticky feeling.

"I don't want to sweat to death before I get to work," she told him as they stood outside underneath the overhang. Both of their cars were sort-of illegally parked there as they had taken advantage of the close-to-the-building, time-limited parking spots.

Tate looked past the excuse Edie made to leave so soon. As she stood there in those red heels, she defined upper class, or just plain classy. Tate was more of a working man in his denim, t-shirt, and Timberlands. They were opposites for certain, but still there was something so obviously alike about them. They looked like a couple.

And they had been quite the pair, until their faults got in the way. Mistakes were made, judgment became too harsh. No one was perfect, and Tate had finally realized that now.

"I know you want to get the hell out of here, and maybe never look back." It was almost painful to know how capable this man was of reading her thoughts. "You've been through hell, and I wasn't there for you. I judged you and I had no right." Edie looked away. She did not want to focus on his understanding and sincerely apologetic words. That was not where this was supposed to lead. She agreed to see his mother today. And it had to end there.

"Thank you for saying that," was all she could manage to say to him. She started to turn on her heels. Tate knew she was pulling away. He realized that sometimes you just cannot go back. What's severed, sadly, cannot be repaired. With every fiber of his being, he didn't want the two of them to be an example of lost love.

"E," he caught her attention before she took the first steps away from him. "Have a drink with me after work tonight? This doesn't have to be over."

She could feel those unshed tears pooling in the back of her eyes. *Don't let him see your pain,* she told herself. *You are Edie Klein. A pillar of strength when most would crumble.* She detested how vulnerable she felt right now with him.

"I can't," she replied, holding herself together.

"Tomorrow night, maybe? I remember your crazy work schedule…" He made light of it now, but they both knew he had a serious problem with Edie choosing to put her career first all of the time.

"I meant I can't, we can't," she tried to clarify. "It's been six months, Tate." As if either of them needed to be reminded.

"Too damn long, if you ask me," he added, feeling as if he needed to hold his breath until she changed her mind, gave in, and said yes to grant them a second chance.

"Long enough for me to learn to let go," she lied. She had to lie. It was easier that way. She could not risk losing him all over again when it would not work out for the two of them a second time. In so many ways, they had been wonderful together. But, there would always be something to get in their way. Edie's worst fear was that she believed Tate would want her to forgive her sister, like she had forgiven his mother. It did not work that way. And there was no chance in hell that she would ever allow Sydney back into her world ever again. Not even Tate could influence her to try.

Tate's heart sank. *She had moved on.*

"Goodbye, Tate." This time, Edie managed to turn on her heels and walk away.

Chapter 22

Tate stood on the curb, watching her pull away. He was parked in front of her so she had backed up her car, shifted it into drive, and sped off. He knew her well. She was in pain. Covering up pain was how she had lived her life. And, now, because he had caused her pain too, she was going to stop at nothing to keep him from hurting her again. He swallowed the lump building in this throat as the unpleasant hot wind blew in his face, shuffling the curls in his hair. If this was the end of them, losing her would most definitely be his biggest regret for as long as he lived. There was just no possible way Tate Ryman could let go of her. That, he knew for certain.

The mental institution allowed visitors every Saturday morning. Even though she was never expecting anyone, Sydney always walked down to the dining area and sat alone at a table in the corner. From there, she people watched. There were families that gathered, and it was refreshing for Sydney to see new faces. She had not perceived herself as crazy. She didn't belong locked up in there. Her case was more like temporary insanity, and she hoped to prove that about herself after she spent the remainder of her sentencing repenting. She had six months down, and one year longer to go. Eighteen months of her life in there seemed like it would be an eternity.

She could have blamed herself for falling in love with Tate Ryman, but there was no way to change how she felt. She wanted to blame her sister, but she had already done enough of that. She didn't long for the day when she would see Tate again, because she knew all too well that never seeing her again would be too soon for him. The last time she saw him, when he knew the truth about her, he could not even look at her. *He must hate her that much.* She knew how hate felt. And she understood how it could slowly eat away at a person's soul.

So what kind of life could she have when the day came for her to be free? Sydney already knew the answer to that. She would seek a fresh start, far from Camden, Delaware and anyone who knew her miserable story.

From afar, Sydney could see more people filing into the dining area. Some of the tables were full, others were not. Sydney wasn't the only one who never received visitors. Many of the patients there were too far gone, like Sydney believed her roommate was. The faces of the visitors were beginning to look familiar to Sydney, but there were always a few new ones, too.

Today, from afar, Sydney could see a wheelchair being pushed. An elderly woman was in it, but Sydney's focus was not on her when she saw the man behind the chair, rolling it closer and closer in Sydney's direction. She was afraid to stare in fear of what she was seeing would disappear. Mrs. Ryman had aged since the incident in her kitchen. Sydney may never have recognized the smaller, frail woman if her son had not been walking behind her chair. *Tate was there.* And the sight of him caught Sydney's breath.

She never said a word as the two of them came to her table. It was Mrs. Ryman who spoke first. Her speech was unusually slow, but clear. "Sydney, dear, I need to speak with you." Tate only stared at her, and when Sydney caught his eye, she blushed profusely and quickly looked away. She suspected that he did not want to talk to her, and had only been there to escort his mother to her. But, what Mrs. Ryman wanted to say to her was beyond Sydney's comprehension.

Tate pulled a chair away from the table, and then carefully guided his mother's wheelchair in its place. "I will be back in one hour," he bent forward and quietly spoke into his mother's ear. Mrs. Ryman only nodded and waited for him to walk a good distance away before she spoke.

Sydney's hands were on the tabletop in front of her, folded and wringing went from sweat. She was a nervous wreck. She had not at all been prepared for this moment. It saddened her that Tate did not utter a single word to her, but she understood why.

Sydney was aware that Mrs. Ryman had been in a coma for several months. There was an article in the Camden News

Leader that she had read about the local business owner of Ry's Market finally on the road to recovery following an accidental overdose. The reporter had been kind with his word choice, although it had been an accident in how Mrs. Ryman ended up drinking the loaded mug of drugs meant for Edie. Sydney knew she was going straight to hell for still wishing her sister had been the one to overdose. She was also sane enough to realize those thoughts were what put her in this place.

"I am not here to judge," Mrs. Ryman began. "I've gone over that edge, too." *What a funny way to phrase it,* Sydney thought.

"Why are you here?" Sydney asked her, and she caught herself purposely speaking slowly, wondering if Mrs. Ryman's comprehension was affected, too.

"To do some good," Mrs. Ryman replied.

"I think you are going to need more than an hour to turn this bad witch into a good one," Sydney stated with excessive sarcasm in her tone.

"I'll be here every Saturday for the next year if that's what it will take," Mrs. Ryman appeared adamant.

"I don't understand," Sydney admitted. "What's done is done. I will serve my time, and be grateful it's in here and not in a prison cell."

"I want to understand you in order to help you," Mrs. Ryman spoke again, and Sydney felt like she was still talking in circles.

"Help me what?" Sydney didn't believe she could be helped. There wasn't anything anyone else could do to reform her. She had lost everything that once mattered to her –her job, her only family, and Tate– all because she had made brainless, insane choices. Choices with dire consequences.

"Find your way," Mrs. Ryman stated.

"And just what direction is my way? Where are you suggesting I go?" Sydney just decided to play along. If Mrs. Ryman was insistent enough to come here today, she deserved Sydney's respect and cooperation.

"Back to your sister." Mrs. Ryman's answer startled Sydney. *Now she was talking crazy again.*

Chapter 23

The hour passed like five minutes, and Sydney surprised herself how much she enjoyed talking to Mrs. Ryman. Maybe it was because, for six months now, there had really been no one to talk to inside of that place. There were three different psychiatrists who had tried to shrink her head, but none of them felt worth delving into her emotions with. It was different with Mrs. Ryman, because she cared.

When Tate came back, on the hour, to get his mother, Sydney thought of how she had not washed her hair in days, and her gray sweatsuit was too snug around the middle. At least the food was worth looking forward to in that facility. She was never a vain woman, like Edie, but Sydney did feel self conscious right now with Tate there. *What did it matter, he can't even look at me anyway.*

"Ready, Ma?" Tate asked, only making eye contact with her.

"Until next week, goodbye Sydney." Sydney reached across the tabletop and patted her aging hand. *Maybe Mrs. Ryman could help her after all.*

Sydney watched the two of them walk away. No, Tate had not looked at her or spoken to her, but he had brought his mother there to see her. That had to mean something. And it did to Sydney.

As soon as the two of them were outside of the facility, Tate spoke for the first time. "Are you sure you want to keep coming back here?"

"I am," she replied. "There is good in that girl, and I know I can help her. I feel compelled to." Mary Lou refrained from saying more. She had told no one that when she had first slipped into a comatose state, her late husband was there. He was the one who encouraged her to go back and help those girls. And to save Tate from a lifetime of unhappiness.

"I couldn't even look at her," Tate admitted, but he really didn't feel ashamed.

"That will take time. She trampled all over your trust." Mrs. Ryman did not fault Tate for how he had handled the entire situation. She did, however, wish he had not thrown Edie out of his life. There was a time when she would have rejoiced at the idea, but not anymore. Not when she recognized how miserable he was without the woman he loved.

"I just don't see how you can help her," Tate stated as they reached the car. He locked her wheelchair with his foot as he prepared to open the passenger door of his truck and then help her up inside of it. It had only been a week since his mother had been home from the hospital. She was slowly resuming her regular lifestyle. The damage to her heart from the overdose was evident. Walking a long distance from the parking lot today would have been too much for her to handle. Still, Tate had high hopes for his mother to make a full recovery. She had been a completely healthy and active seventy-five-year-old woman.

"I believe that she and Edie both have to face their past before they can have a future. Whether that future brings them together or not, I don't know if that really matters. It's just time for them to make peace and stop the destruction within themselves."

Tate shook his head at his mother. "And you're going to try to accomplish all of that on Saturday visits to this place?"

"That, and I want to see Edie again." Tate's eyes widened at the thought, and he kept quiet. His mother would just have to find out for herself how Edie was finished with all of them. And once she made up her mind, she never changed it.

After Tate settled his mother into her house, he waited for the nighttime nurse to arrive before he left. Until his mother was well enough to stay by herself again, Tate had hired nurses to care for her around the clock. Mary Lou objected at first, but then she realized Tate was making it possible for her to go home and live in the house she dearly loved. Given that, she could tolerate a nurse in her home.

Instead of going to his house, Tate drove further into town and stopped at Lantern Inn. He was frequenting that bar more than he had in a couple of years. It was just too quiet at home now. Even when Edie used to work entirely too much and many late nights, Tate never felt as alone as he had in the past six months. At least then she had come home to share their bed. He slept on the couch some nights now, where he fell asleep with the television on. Tate was not going to chase her, nor beg to come back to him. That day outside of the nursing home, he had made his feelings clear. And so had she.

The barroom was only about half full when Tate walked in and took his usual seat on that red barstool with no backing and a generous tear on the side. Bartender Jack knew his story. The whole town did. There had been more than a few women who were interested in snagging Tate Ryman now, but not a one had turned his head.

Tate was chatting with a man sitting beside him at the bar, whose name he didn't know. He was drinking a third beer when the door opened up and he happened to turn his head. It's just what he did sometimes after sitting at the bar for hours. He was never looking for anyone new to meet, to take home. Tate was not that kind of man. At thirty years old, he knew what he wanted. The night of Edie's accident, he bought her a ring. They were supposed to begin the next phase of their lives together then. And then everything unraveled, leaving Tate feeling as if he was starting all over again. But, that's not what he wanted to do. He wanted Edie. He could hardly stand how badly he missed her. Drinking never eased the pain long enough.

An hour earlier, Edie had still been at the office. She and her boss were in a meeting with a client from New York City. Edie had been trying for months to provide the right link between Stockmann Advertising and this man from the big city. Her recent advertising campaign, which she tediously prepared, tore down, and built up again, had finally caught Michael Reid's interest. Enough for him to fly into Dover and meet her, to see and hear more in person.

A handshake between the two of them and Edie's boss had just sealed a two point five million dollar deal. Edie was floating on air, and her boss was twice as high. Edie's boss was a happily married fifty-five-year-old man who rarely missed dinner every night with his wife. When he had employees like Edie, who were willing to work late hours, he had the leisure to go home after an eight-hour day. Tonight, however, it was Edie's boss who suggested they celebrate with their new client over a drink. Her boss lived in Camden, and hoped Michael Reid from New York City wouldn't think he was too good to have a beer in a dive. He had laughed and said he would enjoy it, because he had grown up in a small town and missed the down home feel of it.

It was Edie who immediately wanted to balk. She had to back out of joining them. Lantern Inn was the place where she and Tate met. She had only been there maybe a few times since with him. She couldn't walk back through those doors and not feel the flood of emotion overtake her heart. She was struggling with his memory and their life together. The last thing she wanted to do was take three steps backwards.

"You're coming, right? You can drive Michael or I can, but let's go celebrate before my wife calls to summon me home." They all laughed, and Edie had not spoken up to decline having a drink with them at Lantern Inn. *Of all places.*

Edie ended up driving their new client from Dover to Camden. Business was over for the day, and she could see him relax, sitting in the passenger seat beside her. He told her how he was divorced with two small children, both boys, ages four and six. His wife had wanted out of their marriage, and he admitted to feeling lost without his family. It had been two years since he became a single man again. Edie listened, and Michael talked some more. Ten minutes later, they were following her boss into the back parking lot of Lantern Inn.

"So what's your story?" Michael asked her at what Edie felt like was a bad time. They were preparing to get out of her car. Her boss was already out of his and walking toward them.

"Unattached," she answered quickly, feeling flustered. And it wasn't because of his question. It was because she saw Tate's full-size silver pickup in the parking lot.

※

When Tate turned his head, he saw two men in business suits. They looked out of place for Lantern Inn, which mostly housed men in denim and boots. But, everyone had a right to walk through that door and patronize Jack's bar. It was the woman sandwiched in between those men that instantly caught Tate's eye. Her sleeveless black dress clung to her every curve. Her black stilettos enhanced her already long legs. He didn't need to stare at her body. He had already seen it, and touched every inch of her. It was the look on her face that he stared long at. She wore a smile, her eyes were bright. She had seen him and then looked away. As if he mattered so little to her now.

What Tate didn't know was what Edie had put herself through as she took steps in the parking lot with her colleagues. *You've got this. You are Edie Klein. You know how to handle pain. Conceal it with a smile.*

Tate watched the three of them find a table in the middle of the barroom. He recognized Edie's boss, as he had met him and shared a handshake at least twice at the annual Christmas parties for Stockmann Advertising. It was the other guy that Tate wondered who he was. He wondered if this was business or pleasure for that man. It made him sick to his stomach to think about it really.

Edie's boss had walked up to the bar. He stood next to Tate, seated on the end, but he never recognized him. Jack served him the requested two beers and glass of white wine. The wine was for Edie, as Jack knew all too well.

Tate turned back to the table and saw that man rolling up the sleeves to his white dress shirt, loosening his red tie. He had already taken off his sport coat and hung it on the back of his chair. Edie was engaging in polite conversation with him, as far as Tate could tell. Tate stared long enough to see Edie throw her head back when she laughed at something he had said, then she ran one hand through her long blonde hair, which she was wearing down, covering her shoulders tonight. Even under the dim lights in that bar, Edie shined.

"You're staring," Jack leaned in from overtop the bar and spoke right in Tate's face.

"Fuck you," Tate said back to him. Jack chuckled at first, and then he saw the real pain in his friend's eyes. So he backed off and let him stare.

Edie's boss wasn't finished with his beer when his cell phone rang. He apologized to both Edie and their new client, but his wife needed him at home. Edie smiled. Most people only dream of finding love like that.

"What about my ride to the airport?" Michael asked, knowing his flight was in two hours. Edie felt obligated. But she wished he would choose to take a cab.

"I can either drive you, or call for a taxi," she told him. "Depends on how many more glasses of wine I drink." Both men laughed and Edie tried to pretend she was having a good time. After all, she knew whose eyes were still on her.

One hour passed. Tate kept drinking beer, as Edie continued to drink wine. Every time she wanted another glass, Tate had watched the man, with the sleeves of his white dress shirt rolled back to his elbows and that loosened power red tie, fetch it for her.

"You're drunk," Jack leaned on the bar top and spoke directly in Tate's face again, "and don't say *fuck you*," he added with a chuckle. It's not that he enjoyed seeing Tate go through emotional hell. He just thought it was pretty damn cool to find a love like that in a lifetime. And, later, when the bar closed down, and Tate was the last man drinking in there, Jack would tell him so. And then push him to fight for her.

Chapter 24

I have to go. My flight leaves in an hour. Edie finally heard the words she had waited for the past two and half hours. "Okay," she told him, tipping back the last swallow of wine in her glass. "Will you tell the bartender to put tonight on a tab and I'll catch up with him later?" There was no way in hell that Edie was going to walk up to that bar. She hadn't yet. And Tate was still sitting there, on the end.

RECKLESS

"It's on me," Michael said, as he stood up. And before Edie could thank him, he brushed her bare shoulder with his hand. It was an innocent touch, not at all inappropriate in Edie's mind. But, Tate saw it, and he knew what that guy wanted from her. He also saw that they were preparing to leave, and he could not take the thought plastered all over his mind. *They were going to bed.*

Tate watched him give Jack his credit card at the bar. He was close enough for Tate to touch, or punch in the face, whichever he felt like and the latter was his preference right now. Tate then watched him walk toward the restroom. This was his chance, as Edie had not been left alone all night.

Tate stood up and he felt the beer rush to his bladder. He could piss later. He wanted to talk to Edie before she left. She saw him stand up and begin to walk toward her. She wondered if he was drunk. Tate could handle his beer, and she had never seen him intoxicated. But she had seen him drink one after another tonight. And she also knew how badly he was hurting. Not so much because he wore his feelings on his sleeve, but more so because she felt his pain. Heartache at its best had done a number on both of them.

He reached her table, and she looked up. There had been fleeting eye contact between them all night, but this was the first time Tate had held her eyes with his.

"Hello E..." he said, and she wanted to respond, *don't call me that*, and tell him he lost his right to. But, once again, it had melted her.

"Tate, how are you?" she asked, pressing her lips together to smile.

"Pretty good," he lied. "You?"

"Doing well," she returned a lie.

"I recognized your boss here earlier," Tate stated. "Who's the other one?"

"Michael, meet a friend of mine, Tate," Edie spoke politely as Michael made his way back to the table and Tate tried to hide his disappointment. *He should have known how fast a man can take a leak. He should not have wasted his time with Edie talking about nothing at all.*

Tate shook his hand, and watched Edie stand up and place her designer handbag on her shoulder. And then Tate heard her ask *Michael* if he was ready.

Tate never moved from standing at the table, but the two of them did. Edie had said *goodbye*. The man she was with had spit out a meaningless *nice to meet you.* And then the door closed and they were gone.

In the parking lot, Edie felt a little shaky in her stilettos. The rocks on the ground were partly to blame, as well as the wine in her system that had gone straight to her head. She was looking down at her feet when she heard Michael speak. "Yes, I need a taxi to take me to the airport in Dover. My location is Lantern Inn, downtown Camden."

Edie glanced from the ground up to him. When he ended the call, she spoke. "I could have driven you there."

"I'm actually thinking you should leave your car here and let the taxi driver take you home after he drops me off at the airport," Michael suggested.

"Nonsense, I'm only a little tipsy. Hardly drunk." She smiled, and he returned a sincere look to her.

He stepped toward her then, and she knew he was going to kiss her. This was not what she wanted. She placed both of her hands on his chest, and gently pushed him away. "We work together now, Mr. Reid."

He smiled. "Maybe I should have declined your business offer and taken you to bed instead." Edie laughed, and left his comment or implication at that. Because *that* was all it was. A suggestion from a man who found her attractive. But, she was uninterested.

They stood in the dim lit parking lot, and within minutes a taxi had arrived. She watched him leave, but had not gotten very far in the parking lot before she heard the door of the bar open behind her. It was Tate. He had been watching them the entire time.

"Your friend left?" he asked, feeling some serious hope building up inside of him. He had also seen her reject another man's attempt to get close to her, to kiss her under the dark sky in the parking lot.

"Colleague," she corrected him, wishing she had already made it to her car.

"Right," Tate agreed.

"Tate, I have to go," she told him matter-of-factly.

"You shouldn't be driving back to Dover," he said.

"I will be fine," she stated and believed her own words

because she no longer felt affected by the wine. In fact, she was sober enough to feel the ache in her heart, the one that this man put there. It never helped to see him again.

"Let me drive you," he suggested, and she giggled. "What?" he asked.

"You're hardly a good choice for a designated driver tonight!" she smiled and even in the dark Tate could see she had smiled with her eyes. *God how he missed when her whole face lit up like that.*

"What are we doing apart, Edie?" He just threw it out there. Said the words he was thinking. And then waited for her to come up with the words to tell him one more time. *That's the way it had to be. Suck it up buttercup. Let it go.* Tate believed she was stronger than him. She didn't need him anymore. That's how she wanted him to perceive her. But that was not at all close to the truth.

"I can't do this," she said to him. "I need to go. You need to go. And while we are both going our separate ways, we need to let go of what we shared."

"You mean I need to let go? Because you already have? I know that, Edie. Dammit, I can see that you are not at all affected by us, who we used to be, and what we could still be together. I don't know how in the hell you do it. Please, tell me so I can be a man and, as you say, let go."

Edie was taken aback. This was her chance to ride with it. She had been successful at making Tate believe she was just fine and over them. She should have reached for his hand, or been as bold to give him a quick hug, and then walk away. But, *those tears* never gave her a chance. The tears that always forewarned her of their attempt to surface. There was no warning this time. Just her eyesight blurred from them, and when she blinked they spilled over onto her cheeks. She abruptly brushed them away with her fingers and then the back of her hand. Tate looked just as startled as she felt. He had never seen her cry before. That's an emotion she always forced away or hid from him.

"Edie...are you okay?" he asked her, moving closer.

She looked down and more tears began to freefall. "Ignore me, I'm just feeling emotional. I–" She never got another word out. Tate wiped the remaining tears on her face with his fingers. His touch was electrifying. Another move closer and the palm of his hand was underneath her jawline and his lips met hers. *This was the kiss in the parking lot she wanted. This was the man whose hands on her she welcomed with desire.* She kissed him back, and the two of them were so close not even air could seep between their sealed bodies.

Chapter 25

He knew she wished they would not have done it. He believed she thought they took things too far. That's why, in the parking lot of Lantern Inn last night, Tate had let her go.

Neither one of them had spoken a word after they separated from each other's arms and from a kiss that resurrected an even deeper passion between the two of them. Edie had just gently touched his face and moved her long French-tipped finger nails through the end-of-the-day scruff near his chin. And then she turned and hurried to walk away.

Tate didn't let it end there. He followed her all the way home, until she safely turned her car into the parking lot of her apartment building. And that's when he left. He wondered if Edie had known he followed her. He even hoped for and awaited a late-night text from her after he drove away. There was, in fact, a text written by Edie. But it remained on her phone screen, purposely never sent. It read, *Thank you for safely seeing me home. That's just another thing that's going to make you impossible for me to get over.*

She never sent those words to him. She couldn't. If she had been strong enough to walk away from Tate in that parking lot after sharing a kiss like only he could give her, she would also have to find the courage inside of her to continue on with her life, without him.

Despite a splitting headache, Tate woke up feeling better than he had in several months. Maybe not as soon as he would like, but eventually he was going to get Edie back.

After the fourth consecutive Saturday of showing up at the institution to visit Sydney, Mary Lou was able to walk by herself from the parking lot to the inside of the building. Tate was unsure at first, but his mother insisted. He watched her intently from the driver's seat of his truck, where he promised he would be when she was finished, or beforehand if she needed him. She did fine walking steadily on her own, and Tate felt immense gratitude witnessing how far she had come. His mother was a fighter. But, he feared her fight to change Sydney or to reconcile her with Edie was a losing battle.

Sydney, who always wore that same gray sweatsuit with all-white tennis shoes, stood up from the table in the corner, which had become their usual meeting place every week. She had known Mrs. Ryman was working hard to regain her strength and she was both surprised and happy to see her walking. Sydney only wished she was half as determined as a woman like Mary Lou. Her life had not been about setting goals and pressing forward. She always seemed to be in a rut, and never cared enough to pull herself out of it. Being sentenced to live in a mental institution had not helped her mindset.

"Look at you!" Sydney could not contain her excitement when Mary Lou reached their table. "You didn't overdo it, did you?" Sydney asked, feeling protective of her now. Mary Lou had quickly become a friend, or even *like a mother* to her. She was definitely someone Sydney trusted, and really Mary Lou was her only companion left in her isolated world. Everyone else had kept their distance, assuming she had gone crazy.

"I assure you, I am fine," Mary Lou received both of Sydney's hands in hers and the two of them began to sit down.

"I know you hope to sprinkle peace on the world," Sydney was now comfortable expressing her cynical sense of humor to the friend she had found in Mary Lou, "and while I do doubt any sort of peace will happen in my life, I do want you to know how very much I look forward to and cherish your visits."

Mary Lou smiled. *If only everyone could see in this girl what she did. She was funny, often witty, kind, sensitive, and straightforward.*

"I want to share something with you today that I believe you will appreciate knowing," Mary Lou spoke in a tone so serious that Edie suddenly felt jittery around her. "If you do not, then I'm wrong and we will just move on." That's what Sydney enjoyed about this woman. She never pressured her to feel any certain way about anything they spoke of. "When Tate first introduced me to Edie," the mere mention of her name made Sydney feel tense, "I immediately concluded that I did not like her. Rumors flew in Camden after what happened in my kitchen that day…and most were false. It's not that I did not think she was good enough for my son. It's that she was too good, too much, too into herself and not enough into others, especially Tate. I was wrong. They were quite a match. I had no idea how lost my son would be without her."

"Wait…What?" Sydney interrupted. Mrs. Ryman implied that Tate and Edie were no longer together. Sydney suddenly found herself back there. Back to the person who fed off of her obsession. The one, with blinders on, who believed anything could happen if she wanted it badly enough. "Did Edie leave Tate?"

Mrs. Ryman looked down at her own hands folded on the tabletop. "Several months ago, he was caught up in anger and he ended their relationship. His head is much clearer now. He realizes he was wrong to let her go."

"Unbelievable," Sydney stated, and it was as if she went entirely somewhere else. Mrs. Ryman watched her closely. Sydney was sitting right beside her, but yet she was so far away and lost in her thoughts. And it was obvious what had just happened. Mrs. Ryman knew Sydney had some sort of renewed hope. But, oh my, how it was a false hope.

"You feel invigorated now, don't you?" Mrs. Ryman called her out, and Sydney jumped back to reality. She felt her face flush. No one had ever been able to read her thoughts, especially her darkest. "You think my son is a free man, and when the next eleven months pass in here, you can waltz back into his life and turn his head this time? I have news for you, little lady, you couldn't be more of a Looney Tune if that's where you're allowing your mind to go. You see, my son is not a free man. His heart belongs to your sister, yes it most certainly does. And I'm certain the two of them will find their way back to each other. With our help."

Sydney's mouth dropped. She, too, was going to jump on this blatantly honest bandwagon. "Over my dead body."

"Excuse me?" Mrs. Ryman instantly became upset. *She had not learned her lesson, or repented for her sins.* "Is that really how far you would go?"

"I'm not crazy, if that's what you are implying," Sydney told her, keeping her voice low, "but I would take my own life without a second thought before I would ever help my sister reunite with the man I'll never stop loving."

"You do belong in here then," Mrs. Ryman spoke as she shook her head multiple times. "You've disappointed me."

"What was I supposed to do? Lie to you?" Sydney continued to act unashamed.

"No," Mary Lou replied, "but you do need to stop lying to yourself. My son is here once a week. He sits inside of his truck in the parking lot. He does not want to see you."

"Maybe he is afraid of what might happen if we talked, really talked, like we used to," Sydney spoke, again displaying obvious signs of being detached from reality.

"Sydney…" The way she said her named sounded as if she pitied her. "I want to help you get out of here when your time is up. I think you deserve a second chance to make things right with your life. But, you have to change. You have to face your past and then let it go."

"You have no idea what you're asking of me."

Tate stepped out of his truck when he saw his mother walk outside of the building. There were still ten minutes left in the hour, he noticed when he glanced at his watch.

"Time's up already?" Tate asked his mother as he walked around the front of his truck and opened the passenger door for her.

"I'm afraid I've done all I can do to help her," Mary Lou spoke regretfully, as she allowed Tate to help boost her up onto the truck's seat.

"Really?" Tate asked, as he remained standing by the open door. He had hoped that meant his mother would no longer want a ride every week to this facility. In the beginning, he had promised her because she told him she needed to heal. Befriending Sydney was something she had felt compelled to do. Tate didn't want to be there, and he didn't want his mother there either. He did not trust Sydney. *You don't dial crazy one day and then become perfectly fine the next.* "So you're finished coming here?"

"I will not come back here…alone," Mary Lou leisurely added.

"What? No way. Don't even ask me to. Out of respect for Edie, I refuse to give that girl a second chance." Tate was adamant.

"Not you," she responded. "That girl in there needs her sister. And you're going to help me convince Edie of that."

Chapter 26

No matter how many ways Tate tried to make his mother see that he had no clout with Edie anymore, she insisted he was the one to talk to her, to convince her that Sydney needed her help.

"Why would she even want to help her?" Tate had asked.

"Because they are sisters, the only family each other has," Mary Lou spoke in defense of both of them.

"There is no love lost between them," Tate stressed again.

"I can't give up on this," Mary Lou had sighed, and Tate furrowed his brow.

"What is going on? Why is this so important to you? No offense, Ma, but you never cared about either one of them before." It was time for Tate to know. As Tate drove her home, she told him the story.

At first, he was skeptical, and had said, "First Edie, now you," in a tone that blared of disbelief. But, then, he wanted to hear more. "So Pops wouldn't let you stay with him, huh?"

"He said it was not my time. He convinced me that you needed me," she admitted.

"I do," Tate nodded his head.

"Your father was adamant about me being the one to bring those girls together, or at least to the point of peace. He said if I didn't try, you would suffer. What do you think that means?"

Tate had just shifted his truck into park once he pulled up onto his mother's driveway. "It could have just been a dream, Ma. Don't risk everything on believing you are capable of making something happen that most likely will not. I want Edie back in my life, but trying to talk her into something she wants no part of will only chase her away."

"And just what exactly have you done to make her realize that you are remorseful and want her back in your life?" his mother asked him.

"I've told her exactly how I feel, and I took her in my arms in the back alley of Lantern Inn and kissed her." Tate smiled wide, and his mother chuckled under her breath and muttered something about him being *just like his father*.

"Blame me. Tell her I sent you. Just go to her and talk about this. This will be my last try." On those terms, Tate agreed to make an attempt to talk to Edie.

This wasn't his usual stomping ground, but a gym in Dover twice the size of the one he frequented in Camden was where Tate ended up after two failed attempts to get Edie to text him back, or return his call.

He walked in after he had seen her car in the parking lot. He had been there yesterday and bought a one-month membership. It was a total waste of money, but in order to get in the door when Edie was there, he did it.

In his jeans, t-shirt, and boots, Tate walked into the men's locker room with a backpack slung over his shoulder. He emerged five minutes later, wearing black gym shorts, a red sleeveless shirt, and charcoal gray tennis shoes. His eyes were searching for her as he walked through the gym. It was crowded in there and all he could see were sweaty bodies, some fit, some not. His eyes rushed over the male biceps and sweat-soaked t-shirts. He had never seen more fake boobs in tank tops in his life. At the moment he was considering switching permanently to this gym. Dover was a *bigger* city full of beautiful women. Tate smirked to himself. He was only interested in one beautiful woman. And he had found her.

Against a far wall, which was nothing but windows, he saw her running on the treadmill. Her shorts were black spandex, her tank top was red – just like his own shirt. He smiled at how they had unknowingly dressed alike for the gym. Her hair was tied back in a high ponytail. He stood there for a moment and watched her push herself. The wire from her white earbuds was long and reached on her chest, bouncing off and on it again with every serious stride on the treadmill. Tate chose a treadmill right next to the one Edie was already on. He stood up on it, and she immediately turned her head. He remembered how she used to complain about people working out right next to her. She was a woman who sought space in almost any situation.

She purposely slowed the treadmill as soon as she saw him. He just stood there on the conveyer belt of his machine, smiling. He heard her sigh and watched her slightly shake her head as she pulled just one earbud out of her ear. "What are you doing?"

"Working out," he replied, noticing that the sweat beads that had formed on her neck had begun to trickle down to her cleavage. *God how he wished he was a sweat bead right now.* He pushed his mind far from that thought before he hardened in his loose gym shorts.

"Wrong gym," she told him matter-of-factly.

"Trying something new," he responded.

"I'm on my last mile, and leaving soon," Edie said, as if to forewarn him that she wasn't staying there with him, nor was she in the mood to talk.

"I see," he responded. "Guess I need to get here earlier tomorrow then."

Edie rolled her eyes, and placed the earbud back into her ear before she started up the machine to begin running again. Tate did the same, right beside hers. He purposely ran faster and harder than her. He was a man, trying to show off. He also was in great shape and always did enjoy a good, hard run. Just as much as his girlfriend. And that was the fire inside of him right now. He wanted her to be his again. He missed everything about her. The quirks. The misunderstandings. The drive she had to be the most successful in her career, to look the best in a tight dress. All of it was who Edie Klein was made of, and Tate was so completely in love with her that he couldn't stand the thought of another moment of being apart from her. He only hoped, and sometimes found himself begging God, for her to feel the same again.

When Edie slowed her treadmill to a stop, Tate followed. She removed both of her earbuds simultaneously, letting them drop onto her cleavage. Tate stared for a moment.

"My eyes are up here, hot stuff," she spoke to him, and he laughed out loud, and replied, "I know where everything is." The sexual tension between them was high. Tate, however, felt he was suffering most from it. Edie, as usual, appeared calm and cool. And unaffected by her feelings. *If she was feeling the way he was.*

"You need to carry on with your workout. Don't stop because I'm leaving." Edie told him, as she stepped off of the treadmill. He did the same. Neither one of them paid any attention to the slew of people working out around them.

"Are you going back to work?" he asked her, well aware it was five-thirty in the evening, but also knowing her. Many times she worked late after dinner, or after a workout. He no longer knew her routine though.

"Tate, don't," she said, referring to him wanting to know her business.

"I could tell you the same. Don't. Don't ignore my texts, my phone calls. Please, just hear me out," he stated.

"There were only two," she replied, referring to his attempts to contact her within the last week. Both times he had texted and called her, she felt too weak to respond and was afraid she would give in to him. She had moments of weakness and moments of great strength. Right now, she felt like she could walk away from him.

"Two attempts to get you to listen. Just hear me out. I swear if you want me to walk away after I have my say, I will." Tate wished he had not promised her that, but he was desperate for her attention.

"I will make you live up to that deal," she stated, and he smiled. *That smile, his straight white teeth. The curls in his hair slightly matted with sweat.* Suddenly Edie didn't feel so brave anymore.

Tate nodded his head. There was a café across the street, and she agreed to meet him there in ten minutes.

Tate was already seated outside of the café, underneath an umbrella table for two. He had ordered two bottles of water and an apple for Edie. Following her workout, she always ate a red apple. He didn't know why she did so, he just had known.

He again wore his jeans, a fitted white t-shirt, and boots. He watched her climb out of her car, wearing a yellow sundress and dark brown stilettos. Her hair was pulled up in a knot on top of her head, and she had her large, dark sunglasses on, too, and Tate knew why. Ten minutes was not enough time for her to shower and reapply her makeup after a workout. It didn't matter to him at all. He always believed she was beautiful with or without her face painted.

"I am so going straight home after this," she told him, and he chuckled because he knew her well. *Wearing no makeup made her feel self conscious.* "How bad do I look, really?"

"Do you seriously want me to answer that?" he replied, as she sat down in the chair across from him and he sat again after standing for her. He offered a bottle of water and she took it immediately after she looked down at the apple and smiled. *He remembered.* "You're beautiful. You're always beautiful. And you know it."

She smiled at him again. She missed his straight-from-the-heart compliments. She had taken so much for granted. Especially him. "Thank you," she said, looking down at her French-tipped finger nails wrapped around the water bottle that was sweating on her fingers.

"I came to see you today for two reasons," he began. "One, I want you to know that I'm sorry. You know I want you back, but more than anything I want your forgiveness. I should have believed you, I should have supported you." Edie listened as he concluded his reason number one.

"What's your other reason?" she asked him, trying to conceal how grateful she felt for his words. He wished he could see her eyes behind those large sunglasses right now.

"My mother has been going to visit Syd," he began, and Edie instantly put her guard up. If this conversation was headed in the direction she thought it was, she wanted to be done. Now. "She wants the two of you to talk." Tate waited for the fallout.

"Absolutely not!" Edie voice was loud and then she caught herself. *They were in public.* "She is out of my life, and that's where I want her to stay." Edie paused. She was never going to tell him this. But, now, she knew she had to. "You want me to forgive you? You want me to come back to you? You want to be *us* again? The one thing that has kept me from falling back into everything we used to have and be together, is Syd." Tate didn't understand, but he waited for her to explain. "You will not ever truly get her. You liked her. You pushed me time and again to welcome her into my life. My life with you. You defended her, you took her side when I needed you most." Tate looked down for a moment. He felt such shame. "I get that she blindsided you. What I cannot see, and what I will never open myself up to is having a future with you, without wondering or worrying if you will one day ask me to forgive and forget all that Sydney has done. I won't do it. Not even for you."

Tate sat there in silence, and then finally he spoke to her. "Take off your sunglasses," he requested.

"Why?" She didn't want to.

"I want to see your eyes when I tell you this," he stated, and Edie at first hesitated to remove her sunglasses, but a moment later she did. Her eyes right now looked pained. "Syd deceived me. I do not want her back in my life. If you ever choose to have her back in yours, I would completely understand. I will never ask that of you. My mother, however, has other ideas."

Edie looked puzzled. She didn't understand why his mother had visited Sydney, or why she cared if their relationship was or was not ever rekindled. And Tate tried to shed some light on why his mother was involved. "When Ma overdosed," he said, and Edie cringed because that was another god-awful day in her life, "she slipped into a coma and Pops was there."

Edie's eyes widened. *Not her too?* She could see on Tate's face that he now believed something like that could happen. His mother must have been successful at convincing him, because she never had been.

"Ma wanted to stay with him. She wanted to leave her life behind, and be with him. She wanted to die." Tate sighed. "He told her if she did not go back to try to help you and your sister, my life would never be the same. Ma chose to come back because she thinks she can do some good, maybe make up for the awful thing she tried to do to you."

Edie just wanted to run from all of it, but she knew she couldn't. She owed Tate the truth. "I am so incredibly happy to know that your mother *saw* your father. That's pretty amazing. And I know you believe her. I also understand why you didn't believe me. It seemed so crazy. But, it did happen." Tate nodded his head, and Edie continued to speak. "What seems even crazier to me now is making amends with Syd. I am not safe when she's in my life. So how can you ask me, on behalf of your mother, to put myself in danger again?" The thought terrified her. She was trying to move forward with her life, and now Tate was doing to her exactly what she had feared. Even if it was for his mother.

"I can't," Tate instantly chimed in, and Edie looked surprised at him. "And I won't. You just told me that the real reason why you could not or would not come back to me was because you feared I would push for you to reconcile with Syd. Look, I don't care if you never speak her name again. And I will tell my mother the same. And I'll even send a memo to Pops. I'll tell him that you and your sister do not need to make peace in order for me to be happy and live a fulfilling life. All I need for that – is you."

Edie choked back the lump in her throat. "Go with me," she spoke so softly that Tate had almost not heard her.

"Anywhere," he said to her, as he reached for her hand across the table and it was trembling.

Chapter 27

For as long as Tate lived, he was sure he would never understand women. Especially Edie. She had been adamant about not seeing her sister again. She even had gone as far to admit she chose to stay out of his life in fear of the pressure to do the noble thing and give Sydney a second chance. And, now, she had asked him to go with her to the mental institution. She did not fully explain her reasoning why, and that had made Tate feel more nervous than he was willing to admit. Yet, he wanted to be by Edie's side because she had asked him to be.

They drove in Tate's truck, in silence. Edie asked him not to speak. No more questions about why she so abruptly changed her mind, or what her intentions were now. Edie realized what he was thinking. She had changed her mind so drastically, so suddenly. Even she was afraid to go through with this now. But fear had never stopped her before.

When they reached the institution, Tate parked in the same spot he had for weeks with his mother. He shifted the gear into park and killed the engine. And then he reached for her hand. The sun was beginning to set as they sat in his truck for a moment longer. "Are you sure you want to do this?" he asked her. Edie had called ahead from her cell phone at the café before they both got into Tate's truck. She spoke directly to the administrator, and had been granted permission to visit her sister. Saturday mornings were the only time visitors were allowed, Tate had informed her of that. Edie described her need to be there tonight as an emergency, and so no questions were asked. Camden was a small town. Everyone knew why Sydney Klein was locked up. And everyone felt great sympathy for her successful, beautiful sister who had fallen victim to her madness. Even the administrator of the institution was sympathetic.

Edie sat there, holding Tate's hand. She never before had truly appreciated their bond, their connection, their chemistry, and their passion for each other. If they were meant to have a second chance, Edie knew she would never take him, or them, for granted again.

"I don't want you to leave my side," she spoke, quietly. "No matter what, I want you to stay."

"Okay, I'm here for you," he promised.

"And, please, don't judge me. I cannot help it if she brings out the worst in me." Tate didn't quite fully understand what Edie meant by that comment, but he did nod in agreement because he believed she had every right to be resentful.

※

They walked inside together. Edie would tell him later how much it meant to her to have him with her. Because she was afraid. So fearful that she wondered if she would be able to speak without her voice quivering and her body trembling. But she was determined to do this.

Edie did the talking when she encountered the first employee walking in the foyer, dressed in royal blue scrubs. She asked for the administrator, and stressed that Mr. Seger was expecting her. There were cameras everywhere in that building. The administrator had already seen a beautiful woman walk in with a man by her side. He left his office to meet them.

Tate and Edie both shook his hand. Mr. Seger was a tall man with a large frame and a belly that peeked out of his navy suit coat and hung over the belt of his matching dress pants. "Your sister does not know you are coming, as you requested she was not told. You can find her in the library. There is a private office in the far right corner of the library, you may go in there with her. Be aware that there is a red button on the upper right corner of the inside door frame in that office. If you need help, just press it, and security will be there." Tate and Edie both felt the severity of this place at the same time.

They walked in silence to the library. Neither of them looked around or made eye contact with anyone other than the occasional orderlies in their path. Tate wondered why some of the patients were locked up and others were free to roam. *Maybe they had earned it?* If that was the case, Sydney had earned library time tonight. Perhaps, there, she was perceived as more troubled than dangerous.

Tate saw her first. She again wore a gray sweatsuit, too tight around the middle, and those white tennis shoes with the thick soles. Her once shoulder-length auburn hair had been cut shorter and it was pulled back in a low, tiny ponytail. Her back was to them as she stared up at a row of books on the shelf. Tate pointed silently in the direction of Sydney, about thirty feet away from them. Edie saw her now, too.

"Syd," Edie spoke her name and Sydney instantly jerked her head around. She stared at her sister in a yellow dress. *Her sister's perfection sickened her.* And beside Edie, was Tate. *Her heart would always skip a beat for that man.*

"What are you doing here?" Sydney now turned her back to the books on the shelf, but kept her distance from her sister.

"I came to tell you something," Edie spoke, and Sydney recognized how she showed no emotion. *What else was new,* Sydney thought negatively about her already. Her mind raced for what her sister could possibly have to tell her. Because the two of them were there together, Sydney assumed Tate and Edie were back in each other lives. *If her sister was there to rub that in, she would regret it.*

No one suggested going into the private room. The three of them just stood there, sandwiched between book shelves. Tate stood right beside Edie, but he never spoke.

"I was not going to come here," Edie said pointblank. "I never wanted to see you again." Sydney never flinched. She just stood there and took the beating, as she had so many times with her big sister. Tate almost felt sympathy for her. The look on her face was complete innocence. But, no, he knew better now. That was her look of deceit. "But then I had this revelation. You, imprisoned in this place, have been successful at keeping me from living my life. You were winning." Sydney felt like smirking. She finally had managed to get ahead of Edie. That, alone, had almost made being locked up worth it.

"Careful, Edie. You're the one talking crazy now. You've never let me win." Tate observed the two of them. The animosity had always been there, but it was a thousand times more intense right now. He felt as if something final was going to have to happen between these two. And it worried him.

"No, that's where you're wrong, little sister," Edie told her. "You won that night in the backseat of our parents' car. Don't you remember?"

Sydney's eyes widened. They had never spoken of it. Sydney assumed Edie had not remembered. She was certain she would have confronted her about it. And held it over her head. *Maybe she had? In her own way, she had. Edie's cold-hearted actions and inability to love her were not just from the pain of grief, but the resentment from the way their parents had given in to Sydney, whining in the backseat of their car. The nagging that led to the decision that changed the course of all of their lives.*

Sydney remained quiet.

"I asked you a question. Don't you remember getting your way? We were almost to the movie theater. That late-night Friday movie mama and daddy had promised us for weeks. They were so happy, holding hands in the front seat. We thought it was gross then, but think about it now. To be that in love. I'll bet they would still be so into each other today – if they had lived."

"Why are you doing this? I was just a kid." Sydney did not want to rehash that moment. The moment she wished she could have taken back since she was eleven years old. *But, really, she had not been able to mature or progress since then.*

"You had to have your blankie. The one you were too big for, but couldn't go to sleep without. The same tattered piece of fleece that you never left home without, if it was dark outside. Daddy got angry, and said you were a big girl. Mama never could stand to see you cry. They started arguing in the front seat – over you and your blanket. Daddy eventually gave in, criticizing mama for always taking your side and giving in to her baby. He turned our car around and we headed back home. At the next intersection, daddy never saw that reckless car speeding through the red light, coming right toward us. No, he wasn't watching the road. He had been looking in his review mirror at you, still screaming your head off like a baby even though we were going back for your fucking blanket."

Tears were streaming down Sydney's face. Tate was staring at them both in disbelief. He had never heard any of this before. They were just kids, doing mindless things to get their way. No one should have to pay for the rest of their lives for a moment that should have been a distant memory, or mocked with laughter many years later.

"You ruined that blanket afterward," Sydney accused her.

"No, you did," Edie corrected her. "I caught you sleep walking into the kitchen when we were living back in our house with our aunt who eventually couldn't take your craziness. "You cut it, every inch of it with a scissors. It was in shreds. The scissors was in your hand. And yet you blamed me."

"I don't remember that," Sydney spat at her. "But I do remember bringing it into the backseat of the car that night. I had it placed between us. I know I did."

"We lost our parents that night over a blanket," Edie told her, and Sydney flinched.

"So you've blamed me for that all of these years. That's why you said you never wanted to speak of our parents or what happened ever again. You hated me for it." An outsider would have seen this as utterly ridiculous. But, Tate didn't. He stood there, taking in all of it. And he hoped the truth would set them both free.

"I hated myself more," Edie admitted, and Sydney looked perplexed. "I didn't want to go to the movie that night. I was a teenager, who didn't want to be seen with parents and a little sister. Mama would never let me go to the late night movie, but I knew some of my friends were going to be there. And here I was going to show up, like a dork, with my family." Edie paused before she continued. "I was sitting on your blanket. It was balled up under my leg."

Chapter 28

Sydney gasped, and then she blurted out, "Noooooo!" as Edie only stared at her. She dropped to her knees. And clenched the sides of her hair that had been pulled back into a ponytail that was too small to bother. The truth had sent her over the edge. She began ripping out her own hair, and then she turned around and started to destroy the bookshelf, recklessly throwing books everywhere. She especially focused on hurling them at Edie. *Her sister had allowed her to blame herself all of her life for their parents' deaths. Edie's years of silence had forced Sydney to self destruct. She had gone on believing the fault was entirely hers. And no one had helped her to see otherwise.*

Her screams and destruction alarmed the staff while she was being watched on camera. The communication between sisters had ceased. Edie had backed up against the bookcase, opposite of Sydney. She never ran to her, she never attempted to reach her. Tate pulled her close to him as they watched Sydney eventually be sedated with a syringe by two staff members, dressed in all white clothing, who forcefully held her down on the floor.

When she was wheeled away on a stretcher, her eyes were closed. It was then that Edie finally was able to breathe. Tate rushed her outside of that facility, brushing off and ignoring anyone who attempted to approach them as they walked swiftly through those corridors and finally reached the exit. An alarm sounded as Tate pushed open the door without punching in a code, something that he once remembered his mother mentioning. The outside air was cool and they both felt relieved to be in it. They stood in the middle of the vacant parking lot, near Tate's truck.

"I know she will now dwell on this as being my fault, because I let her go on believing it was hers," Edie began speaking, quietly, with her arms crossed as she stood under the dark sky with him. She had chill bumps on her bare arms from the night air, or possibly from the intensity rushing through her body still. That scene inside of there had been a nightmare. No matter how much Edie loathed her sister, this obviously pained her.

"I know you must feel shocked, or even somewhat deceived in all of this," Edie told him, trying to see his face in the dark, to read his emotions. "I've gone through many stages of blame over this. It was her fault. It was my fault. It was our mother's fault for never having a backbone. It was our father's fault for not watching the road, and keeping us all safe. The truth is it was a tragedy. An accident out of our control."

"I don't think Syd will ever see it that way," Tate spoke, carefully. Finally, he understood.

"That's why I asked you to come here with me. No one has ever truly seen it. I've been viewed as the forward bitch, and she as the innocent introvert. She's mentally ill, Tate. She'll never see anything in a healthy way. Her jealously for me turned into crazy hate. Her positive feelings for you turned into obsession. Distancing myself from Sydney has been the only way for me to survive. She feeds off of dwelling on unhealthy feelings. Now, do you see why I cannot have her in my life?"

Tate sighed. "There was so much more to you than I ever realized."

"So much that I didn't want you to see," she told him, realizing how impossible it could be now for them find their way back to each other. If that's what they both even wanted anymore.

"You're a complicated woman," he said, and Edie was not sure if he believed that was a positive thing. *Was she someone he wanted in his life anymore?* He was a good ole boy, a straight arrow. Not perfect, but close, in her eyes. And here she was, wanting to fit seamlessly into his life with her imperfections and all. Edie almost felt foolish for believing in them after so much had come full circle tonight. She had proven that her sister was crazy. And Edie had also shown Tate her greatest imperfection. She was incapable of love.

"I don't know what to say to that," she admitted, looking down at the ground in the pitch dark. There was only one pole light, high above them right now, and she could see Tate's face from its illumination when she looked up again.

"You caught my eye from the first moment I saw you," Tate began. "Your beauty is striking. But, there's more. Underneath it all, beneath what every woman envies and every man wants, you are a wounded soul. You've experience more hurt than anyone should ever have to go through, as a child and as an adult who continued to paint over the pain. You don't have to do that with me anymore. E, I know you, the real you." Tate regretted the times he judged her now more than ever. "And I also know I do not want to spend another second of my life without you in it."

Maybe because it was dark, or perhaps it was how she just knew she could finally be real with him. Whatever the case, Edie had allowed the tears to be free. "You don't have to be afraid to feel anymore," Tate said, reaching for her. He gently placed the palm of his hand on the side of her cheek and it was now wet with tears.

"I know," she said, through those tears. "You've taught me that. I get it now."

Tate reached for her hand and pulled her toward him. He held her close underneath the stars in the sky. He wanted to promise to protect her for the rest of their lives. He wanted to kiss her until they were both breathless. But, he knew what she needed right now was simply the comfort of being in his arms, and the reassurance that everything was going to be okay.

Chapter 29

Her room was dark, her roommate was sleeping. She was always sleeping. The medical staff had thought Sydney, too, would sleep off her drugs. But she was already awake and out of bed. Medication never did affect her much. Dosages had to be doubled or even tripled to take effect.

She stepped over to the window and looked out. Five stories up. The only two people under that pole lamp in the middle of the parking lot immediately caught her eye. Tate was holding Edie. Loving Edie. Moving on with his life without her. *We were supposed to be together...*

And that was the very last thought Sydney had before she opened the window. It had bars on it to keep her and her roommate from doing anything foolish. Only those bars weren't securely intact anymore. Sydney had stolen a razor blade from the bathroom several months ago. After numerous evaluations, the trained professionals there had believed Sydney would never hurt herself, nor ever attempt to escape.

She had nothing else to do, day in and day out. She would sit by the window to get some fresh air, she had told the staff, time and again. But, really, she had been slowly chipping away at the wood on the window sill that had kept those bars safely in place. This was an old building. Some of its wood was rotting internally. Sydney's mission had taken time and patience, but she had managed to work loose two of those bars at the base of the window. The wood crumbled and then broke away as she now pulled hard on both of those bars until they were free and in her hands. She then placed them at her feet on the floor.

She lifted her legs up there first, swung them over what was left of the wood window sill, and then dangled them out into the night air. The sight of those two. *Together.* That was the last thing Sydney saw before she jumped out of that fifth story window.

Mrs. Ryman was sound asleep in her bedroom, lying on her side of the queen-size bed she shared with her husband for forty-eight years. She always drifted off to sleep, hoping to see him in her dreams. Especially since she shared the encounter with him on *the other side*. She believed there was a hereafter, and when it was her time, she would be ready. Missing her husband still consumed her, but she was trying. Focusing on Sydney for all of those weeks had helped, but now Tate had told her to stay away from her. And she believed he was right. *That girl did not want to be helped.*

In her dream, Mrs. Ryman could see clearly herself inside of their market. Tommy Kampwerth was stocking shelves in aisle three again. Everywhere she turned, there was someone else she recognized. Old friends, family members. Some already deceased, some not. She was certain her husband would be around the next corner. This was one of those dreams where she felt awake, and almost in control of the next vision in her mind.

Tate and Edie were walking hand-in-hand. Mary Lou had not remembered a time when she had ever witnessed them being that close and touching. They looked happy, so she in turn felt happiness for them.

The next thing she knew, she had somehow transitioned from walking through the aisles of her store, back to the register near aisle three. *Back to where this dream started*, she comprehended. And then she looked up at the cashier, waiting for her.

"Sydney..." Mary Lou spoke in a motherly tone. She still thought so much of this girl, despite the demons she struggled to overcome.

"Mrs. Ryman, you look beautiful, my friend," Sydney had said to her with one of the most sincere smiles she had ever worn. "Just know... I am all right."

"You are?" Mrs. Ryman asked her, feeling hopeful.

"There's serenity. There's harmony. I am finally all right," Sydney repeated, and Mrs. Ryman opened her eyes. She laid very still in her bed, vividly remembering her dream. And wondering the deeper meaning of it.

It was hours later before Tate was able to get Edie away from that tragic scene. The paramedics, the administration and staff, and the police detectives all had wanted a piece of her time. There were offered words of sympathy, and questions – one after another. Tate and Edie were told this apparently had been a long time coming, a plan of Sydney's, as evidence of the destroyed wood that held the bars in place had been discovered in her room on the fifth floor of that old building.

When Tate brought Edie home, she was completely silent. He let her have that time. She had spoken enough about seeing her sister jump to her death. The sun was dawning as they walked together into the mudroom. Edie took slow, short steps in there. It had been a long time since she had felt like she was *home*. She stopped and sat down on the top step.

"Hey, that's my spot..." Tate quietly teased her.

"I've missed it. All of this. Seeing you sit here. Coming home to this house." She smiled softly, and her eyes were red and swollen from crying hysterically on the ground next to her sister's broken body. Tate could not get that image out of his mind. But, now, he wanted to focus on Edie wanting to be back there. Back home. With him.

"I'm happy to hear that. So unbelievably happy," Tate sat down close beside her, and put an arm around her. "But I'm terribly sad, too," he added. "It didn't have to end this way. She didn't have to–"

"I feel like I gave her the final push," Edie interrupted. "She was barely hanging on, and I shoved her off of the edge."

"Sometimes people do not want to be saved," Tate spoke calmly. He was not going to allow Edie to self destruct over something her sister decided to do a long time ago, all those months back when she was locked up because of her own insane choices. "I think you were her excuse all along. Don't let her bring you down, don't let her sink you into that quicksand. You're bigger than that. A stronger soul than she ever was."

"Do you think she went straight to the fires of hell?" Edie asked, fearing that for her sister.

"No," Tate answered, feeling steadfast in what he believed. "I think there was so much good in her. I saw it. My mother saw it. Those loyal customers at Ry's did as well. And, I know, you also may have caught a glimpse of good once upon a time."

Edie looked down at their feet on the step below from where they sat. Tate turned to her then, and gently placed his fingers underneath her chin that was now quivering. He made her look eye-to-eye with him at this moment. "Say what it is that you are feeling. It's okay. You are safe with me now."

She almost could not see him through the tears that flooded her eyes. "I..." she began, and then choked on a sob. "I...loved her." *Despite everything.*

Tate never expected to hear those words from Edie. He could have cried with her at that moment, but he chose to be strong and fold her up in his arms while she sobbed. *There was no greater pain than knowing sometimes it was too late to fix things.*

They showered, and drank two cups of coffee. Edie didn't have any extra clothes there, so she had slipped into a pair of Tate's drawstring red gym shorts and wore a white t-shirt that he said was too small for him. Her wet hair was past her shoulders, and halfway down her back. She, for once in her life, had not cared how she looked. She was only focused on how she felt. And she answered Tate when he asked again.

"Defeated," she said, honestly. "I always tried to succeed at staying one step ahead of her. Well, she won last night."

"You really think so?" Tate asked her, sitting at the kitchen table with her, bare-chested and barefoot in a pair of jeans. The curls in his hair were also still wet from the shower. "She just couldn't do it anymore, E. Her biggest battle was within herself. It's okay to say she did what she felt she had to do to escape that, that feeling which we know overwhelmed her and forced her to become someone crazy and evil at times. We have to understand where she was coming from. She deserves that now. She's gone. Let's hope she will find peace."

"What you just said makes absolute sense. I need to wrap my mind around that and hold it there. I owe Syd that. I owe myself the peace that I will get ... if I forgive her." Edie words were so sincere she even surprised herself.

"I'm really proud of you right now," Tate spoke softly to her as he leaned in and stole a light kiss on her lips. The gesture was over so quickly that Edie ached. For more.

"I don't know if I deserve that," she told him. "I know there was a time when I was not worthy of your love either." Tate shook his head, but Edie kept talking to him. "I wanted you in my life. I wanted to share this house with you. Your bed, our bed, was a place I've never felt so wanted, adored, appreciated, worshipped, and loved. Never before has anyone ever loved me the way you have. And here I was, this woman you were giving your heart to…and I couldn't even say it." Tate listened raptly. He wanted this, waited for this, more than she would ever know. "I felt it though," Edie forced back her tears to be able to speak clearly to him. She wanted Tate Ryman to hear every single word.

"I love you."

She stood up and sat back down again on his lap. He held her close and he wore a smile that lit up his entire face, while he whispered, "I've always known." And then she kissed him first. She initiated a kiss that sent them both reeling back into their passion that had never simmered down.

Chapter 30

They pried their bodies apart, right there in the kitchen where they had made passionate love countless times. He wanted her. She wanted him. But, first, they knew where they needed to be.

They laughed at how ridiculous she felt wearing his clothes, but she had put a bra back on to wear underneath his white t-shirt. *What would his mother think otherwise?* Because that was where they were going. The terrible news would travel fast in their small town. And both Tate and Edie were worried about how she was going to handle it.

Of all places. Of all things she could be doing. Mrs. Ryman was seated at her kitchen table, drinking a cup of coffee. Tate led the way in front of Edie, and he glanced back at her, knowing what she would be thinking. "Hi Ma," he said, as Mrs. Ryman felt pure joy to see them together. She could only hope for what this meant.

"Tate, honey, I wish you had called if you were bringing company." She ran her fingers through her bedhead and tightened her robe across her chest.

"Ma, it's Edie. It's okay." He wanted to say she's like family and would be family one day because as soon as he got her back home later, he was going to take that ring out of his dresser drawer and out of that little black box it had been stored in for far too long. And ask her to be his wife. To spend the rest of forever with him. Loving him. *She loved him!*

Edie sat down at the far end of the table, partly because she wanted to hide her oversized men's clothing, and otherwise because this was Tate's place. She was only there to offer moral support.

Tate sat in a chair closer to his mother. "Have you seen the news or read the paper yet today?"

"No, but you only ask me that when something bad has happened. Tell me. I'm a big girl," his mother spoke, and Edie felt like saying yes but even the biggest, most courageous human beings still felt pain. And this was going to hurt.

"Edie and I went to see Syd last night," Tate revealed.

"Oh," Mrs. Ryman sighed pleasantly. "I am so relieved to hear that." She focused on Edie. "There is good in that girl. You will see it, too," she told Edie directly, and Tate was quick to interrupt.

"Ma," he caught her attention. "It didn't go well. Sydney has been toxic in Edie's life for a very long time. They've both made mistakes, but their relationship just wasn't meant to be. Edie knows that and I know it now. We have to tell you something. Something happened as we were leaving."

"My sister," Edie began to speak. She did feel like it was her place now, to tell her. Edie's hands were trembling, folded on the tabletop. "She's gone. She took her own life."

Mrs. Ryman gasped and tears sprung to her eyes. She could see the pain, so evident on Edie's pale face and in her red eyes. This girl had no one left in this world – in a life sometimes filled with too much pain and loneliness. She had covered up her emotions so well. Too well. It was time she knew what it felt like to truly be loved again. Tate had already come through. Now it was his mother's turn.

Mrs. Ryman stood up from her end of the table and walked barefoot in her pale pink robe. Edie sat up straight to her full height when she reached her side. "I'm so sorry," she spoke, and Edie nodded. *Was it okay to say thank you? She and Sydney had been lost to each other for half of their lives. Could she really accept sympathy for that loss now?*

"I had a dream last night," Mrs. Ryman spoke, and in no uncertain terms she now realized the message, the meaning behind that dream. "I was at our market…and Sydney was there. She was our cashier again. She told me, and I remember her words so clearly, "There's serenity. There's harmony. I am finally all right. Just know I am all right." I woke up from that dream, trying to decipher it. I now know what it meant."

Edie sat there, taking in every word. She not only believed this, she felt a wave of peace wash over her. Mrs. Ryman had given her that. They embraced, like two close friends, or a mother and daughter would.

Tate sat there, witnessing another close moment between the two women he loved most in this world. And he knew this was just the beginning of their happiness – and their love.

ABOUT THE AUTHOR

Yes, this was a crazy plot. No, there was not one particular moment of inspiration in my own life for this story. But I do, after 41 years, have the experience and knowledge of relationships. What makes them flourish? What causes them to fail? And how do we know when to stop trying, or try harder?

I've learned that everything eventually works out. Maybe not the way we hoped or prayed for, but just how it is supposed to be. How we deal with, appreciate, and accept life and its amazing moments as well as the hardships will mold us into the people we are.

However - sometimes it's too much. The storm is too strong. The pain is too great. Someone or something will be entirely out of reach. Never measure a person's strength. Never judge. We don't know what others endure. And if you do know, reach out. But if your efforts fail to help, it's okay.

As always, thank you for reading!

love & peace,

Lori Bell